CRIMSON CUTLASS & CHAMELEON

The Cabinet of Dr. Faustus

A WARBIRDS OF MARS TALE

By
Scott P. 'Doc' Vaughn

Published by Paperstreet Entertainment, LLC
paperstreetent.com
Glendale, Arizona
2018

This is a work of fiction. Names, characters, places and incidents are products of the authors' imagination or are used fictitiously and should not be construed as real. Any resemblance to actual events, locales, organizations or persons, living or dead, is entirely coincidental.

Characters and concepts copyright © 2018 by Scott P. Vaughn.

Cover art and design copyright © 2018 by Scott P. Vaughn.

Title page logo and illustration copyright © 2017 by Scott P. Vaughn.

Interior Design by Tell-Tale Press
    www.telltalepress.net

All rights reserved.

No part of this book may be used or reproduced in any manner whatsoever without written permission, except in the case of brief quotations embodied in critical articles and reviews.

For information address Scott Vaughn at m-n-v-who@juno.com

Visit Warbirds of Mars on the World Wide Web at:
www.warbirdsofmars.com

Also by Scott P. Vaughn:
Tales of the Hero-Lore
Slaves of Shebwai (writing as Scarlett Vaughn)
Shards of Destiny (coming 2018)
'55 Zombie printed comic (coming 2018)

Also by Scott P. Vaughn and Kane Gilmour:
Warbirds of Mars ongoing webcomic (http://www.warbirdsofmars.com)
Warbirds of Mars printed comic, issue #1
Warbirds of Mars printed comic, issue #2
Warbirds of Mars: Stories of the Fight! Anthology
Warbirds of Mars: The Golden Age printed comic

Acknowledgements

As this particular tome took longer to see fruition than expected, I have a small list of acknowledgments. Thusly I wish to extend the proverbial wave of gratitude to: Kane and Mike, Ang and Erica, Max and my folks, the M&Vers, Andrea, Grace, the Warbirds supporters, the Paperstreet supporters, and of course my cat, Dalton.

-Doc
August 2018

Chapter 1

The haze of a blue tinted moon filtered through the large, glass skylight. It washed over an exotic Chicago penthouse and mingled with the orange illumination of candles and hearth. The glow fell upon the dark hair and soft flesh of Genevieve Marigold Donovan, wealthy heiress of the famous globetrotting Donovans - their only daughter. Her youthful, exotic features were set in a hard mask of contemplation.

Genevieve's short, satin robe did little to hide the tanned skin of her long, shapely legs. She folded them into another yoga position, changing *asanas* for the third time in five minutes. Her meditation was troubled, and the young woman resisted the urge to glance at the glass fixture high above her; she had a nagging fear that unwanted eyes were roving over her body.

The Victrola next to the crackling fireplace was playing a selection of traditional Asian music; its somber strings whispered the tales of a dead Chinese princess. Genevieve ignored the calming tune, returning her thoughts instead to the previous night's events. She was uncertain just how to proceed; a part of her wanted to go out that evening, but perhaps it was better to lay low for a night. Considering the way the local mob had threatened her life only a day before, Genevieve found herself at a crossroads; they had never gotten that close before. It made her work harder, to say the least. But, she mused, one must get back on the horse. Anxiously her thoughts corkscrewed into a mire of self-doubt and fear. The answer was in the next room; she had but to open the cabinet her father had left for her and go out into the dangerous Chicago night air once more, or stay holed up in her condo and pace the room in panic over what to do next.

Genevieve sighed and got up long enough to pick the needle off the record and return the room to silence. Gazing about her own apartments, she took in the scene. The room was dark, lit now by the full moon and the dying fire. African masks adorned the walls between paintings of European courtesans and Japanese scrolls. The shadows kept their secrets, but nothing stirred, and Genevieve assuaged her childish fears with a shake of her brunette curls. Lithe and elegant as a ballerina, Genevieve tipped her body over into a handstand atop an immense fur rug made from the tiger her father had killed in India. She lowered her shoulders to the rug and pointed her toes towards the ceiling, heedless of the way her robe fell away to reveal the silk and lace of her underthings.

Something made a sound at the glass of the skylight. Genevieve rolled from the pose and paused to listen, her heart rate increasing at the thought that perhaps her fears of being watched held merit. Once more her dark eyes scanned the spacious room, but no further noise greeted her except the ticking of the grandfather clock and the pop of dying embers.

She realized that she had landed in a crouch atop the dead tiger's snarling head, so Genevieve stood up with a laugh and smoothed her robe, deciding at last that she had become entirely too paranoid for her age. She was approaching thirty after all, and a lady of her stature would normally have a husband to massage away her fears on such nights. Her days of travel curtailed, she began to wonder whether or not she would ever have the time for such romances. Other duties had called to her since the Great Depression had enveloped her homeland. Chicago had become a hotbed of crime and suffering that she could only do her best to help alleviate.

Genevieve wondered again whether or not she should go out that evening as she had originally planned. Should she face her fears or let the heat cool down for a night? Should she grapple with death in the vain hope of helping the innocent once more? She gazed at the wood-paneled wall, thinking of the ornate, mysterious cabinet in the room beyond. The object that just a few years before had seemed like the answer to such questions was now the source of her apprehension. But she couldn't let fear stop her, Genevieve decided; she had to do what was right in her heart.

There was a sound of breaking glass from above. The young woman gasped in surprise at the disturbing sound and clutched her small robe around her form.

A small metal device made a thud when it hit the tiger rug at Genevieve's feet. In an instant it was spewing a noxious, inky gas into the room. She coughed and stepped back, and out of the shadows a pair of black-clad arms clasped around her like a vice. Genevieve recoiled instantly and tried to twist from the arms holding her. The gloved fingers slipped, grasping at her satin robe. She pulled away and the robe tore, exposing her bare skin and the frayed lace of her brassier.

Genevieve turned, slipping out of his grip and aiming the heel of her hand at her attacker. The figure ducked, and her hand sailed over a hooded face covered by some sort of gas mask and a set of strange goggles. Instinctively she raised her right knee and caught him in the throat, bringing her elbow back down to knock the gagging villain sideways. She spun around and tossed the shredded robe aside, then reached for the mask of her attacker to use in fleeing the smoky room.

Before she could don the mask, something kicked Genevieve's feet out from under her. She landed hard but rolled over and came back up in a fighting stance. She wasn't about to go out without showing these blackguards a thing or two of the martial arts she'd picked up in her worldly travels.

Two more identically dressed figures were stepping through the spreading smoke, their hands outstretched to subdue her.

"Oh," Genevieve said, "that's just not fair."

A fourth assailant appeared behind her, grabbing Genevieve's arms and pulling them behind her back. She heard more cloth tear and screamed, more out of frustration and surprise than fear, which she found strangely interesting given the overthought she had just been giving such scenarios.

But she did begin to feel dread when she realized that the other two attackers were on her as well. Hot hands pawed at her flesh through leather gloves, holding her down.

And when she could smell the chloroform on the rag one of them placed over her mouth, Genevieve Donovan felt panic for the first time since India.

⁓

The skylight shattered as a thug with his load of gas bombs fell through. The black-garbed villain barely had a moment to scream before his body met the floor with a sickening crack, breaking his neck.

The hand at Genevieve's mouth slipped aside and she twisted away from the figure behind her. The other two men turned to see what had happened to their comrade, giving Genevieve the chance to break from their grip and roll aside. She found the mask she had intended to procure beneath her hip and put it to her face, begging her naked limbs to obey her orders and flee the scene. When she found herself still feeble and recovering from the gas attack, Genevieve's heavily-lid eyes peered through the haze to see what had saved her from imminent doom.

The room was awash in gray mist. Genevieve could barely make out the closest furniture between the silver hue of the moon and the orange embers of dying fire. Beyond the shadowy outlines of her attackers a figure dropped into view. The sound of a man descending a silken rope with speed and agility preceded the light thud of his boots landing on the floor. Glass cracked under his heels as this new black shape stood before them all, different than the others though just as ominous.

"Conclave of the Three," he commanded. His voice was deep, and Genevieve found her hand clutched to her breast.

He stepped from the mist to reveal a broad-shouldered man in a long, dark greatcoat and tricorne hat. A scarf or mask covered his features except for his eyes, which were sinister and creased with fury. He pulled a long blade from the scabbard secured to a wide leather baldric and brandished the sword at the villains before him. He twisted it a few times so that they might see the ruby secured in its cupped hilt, or perhaps he was simply keen to show off the width of the steel. With his other hand he aimed a large, multi-barreled weapon, not unlike a pirate's pistol, but larger and with hints of industrialized technology. He raised the strange gun and glared at the men over its springs and bolts.

"The Crimson Cutlass has come for you all," he said. "Surrender or die."

The closest of the Conclave members feigned a forward attack, letting the man to his right instead bolt forward and attempt to land a punch. The figure calling himself the Crimson Cutlass lashed out faster, raking his sword across the man's ribs. The first one had pulled a knife and closed in for the kill, and Crimson's pistol fired, but the shot missed and the two began to grapple.

Genevieve shook her head once more, trying to clear it. Her hand felt for the wall behind her, searching for the hidden catch while she watched to make sure the others were all too busy to notice. The wealthy heiress heard a slight tap as the catch depressed. She smiled and rolled backwards, disappearing through the trap door in the wall and letting it close silently behind her.

∾

The costumed man known as the Crimson Cutlass wore two masks; the scarf covering his face and the mask of rage and hate for oppression. The second one dropped momentarily when he saw the lithe girl he had come to rescue suddenly summersault backwards and disappear through a wall.

"Oh, that's just not fair," he mumbled to himself.

But he had bigger fish to fry.

His arms were occupied with blocking both the knife and the blackjack his opponent had tried to bring to bear, so he kicked out with one leather boot and sent the villain reeling. Crimson had barely a second to respond to the third assailant that flew at him out of the mist, but he brought his pistol to bear in time and squeezed off a shot that took him in the chest. The black-clad man dropped with no more than a gasp before Crimson's pistol had even rotated the barrel and fed another round into the chamber.

"One," he said.

A gloved hand whisked out of the darkness, a knife flashing briefly where Crimson had just been standing. He answered with a swipe of his own blade, hacking the member of the Conclave of Three down where he stood. The failed assassin screamed once and fell twitching.

"Two."

Before he could turn the sword was kicked out of his hand. Crimson twisted around, trying to bring his pistol into play once more, but the last of the attackers had gripped him in a sort of sleeper hold. His legs were swept out from beneath him and they both went to the floor in a heap. Stunned, he shook his head to clear it, only to find the Conclave member that had felled him was now kneeling before him, dagger drawn to Crimson's chest. The weapon was poised to sink deep, piercing his heart and quickly ending Crimson's life. The assassin smiled.

Something - an unseen force of some kind - slammed into the killer's side before he could deliver the blow. The Conclave member turned and slashed, his knife passing through empty air. Despite this, a second blow struck him, doubling him over. Crimson observed a slight flutter in the air, like a shimmering mirage or curtain of warped light that made the wisps of nearby smoke dissipate.

Someone was there, and they were invisible.

A third punch landed, striking the assassin in the face. He went down at last, knocked cold. The shimmering effect moved the air over him momentarily, then went still. The Crimson Cutlass felt his own expression change openly from disbelief over his luck, to that of wry calculation. With one leg he kicked out, sweeping the area in front of him. The kick connected with an unseen ankle and a gasp of surprise preceded a thud to the floor. The figure had gone down.

And when they did, their invisible cloak fell aside.

Dark lashes behind a masked visage locked eyes with his own; a lithe figure froze and gazed at him in surprise. The black, hooded cloak - no longer invisible - had concealed a simple dark evening gown and corset, a pair of opera gloves, and midnight curls. A shred of white silk peaked out from the generous bust line, confirming what the Crimson Cutlass had already deduced; that the beautiful girl and invisible savior was also the very same heiress he had arrived to rescue.

"Well, well," Crimson smirked. "This *is* a surprise; the Chameleon, I presume." His eyes darted briefly to the expanse of long legs revealed by her prone form and the slit along her dress. He looked away out of respect, but she had already noticed, and covered the torn undergarments with the cloak. Crimson stood and offered her his hand to help her stand, but she refused. "Sorry about the mess," he told her.

"Did you have to do that?"

Crimson tried to look briefly sheepish. "Well, I was curious – there appeared to be an invisible woman in the room, so I tripped her."

"No," Chameleon answered. She pointed disapprovingly to the bodies littered among the broken glass on her floor. "That."

He raised an eyebrow. "I should think Genevieve Donovan can afford the cleaning bill." He tried not to smirk at his own cleverness, though he failed.

The Chameleon sighed in resignation. "I meant killing them." She unhooked a looped bullwhip from her hip and knelt down to inspect the one she had felled, turning the unconscious man's head to one side to inspect his features or health, Crimson was uncertain which.

With that, the Crimson Cutlass was back in full character again. He knelt beside the surprising girl he had come to rescue, gesturing towards the prone villain. "They're called the Conclave of the Three," he said, pointing at the figure's strange mask with its three dots on the side of his goggled helmet. "They're a secret organization of murderers with a global agenda and ties to the Nazi party. They came here to kill you - or capture you, I'm unsure which. They were also here to steal something."

At that, Chameleon looked at him and stood up. She walked resolutely to the wall she had disappeared through before and maneuvered it open. Reaching inside briefly she found a length of rope and threw it to her would-be savior. "Tie him up, then follow me," she said, and entered the secret room.

"Ma'am," he answered, with a slight tip of his tricorne hat. He turned the surviving Conclave member over to bind his hands behind his back. He glanced around the room briefly before activating a small device on an ornate bracelet on his left wrist. A false ruby at the center of the golden wristband began to pulse with a steady light. "Where's your house servant?" he called to her.

"I let her have the evening off," came the answer from the hidden room.

The panel leading to the Chameleon's secret room was still slid open, so Crimson ducked inside. In the dark he came suddenly face to face with the girl.

"Oh," she said, her long lashes fluttering momentarily behind her black domino mask.

Crimson couldn't help but smile, though he hoped it was more charming than he suddenly felt. "Oh, hello." He couldn't take his eyes from hers. "It's darker in here than I'd suspected."

"I - I was just about to light my candles," Chameleon stammered in apology. She lowered her eyes and her hood, removing her mask. The beautiful heiress, Genevieve Donovan stood before him in her tight gown and strange cloak, but only briefly. She adjusted the mask and placed it back on. "I was in such a hurry to get back in the fight that I could barely see out of this thing. You're the first 'costumed hero' like myself that I've ever met."

Crimson nodded in conceit. "Chicago could do with a few more with your courage and beauty. Er, resourcefulness, I mean." She smiled a little at his befuddlement. "Though I'm surprised at your squeamishness. I have heard that the deaths of at least two mobsters can be laid at the Chameleon's door."

She began lighting candles, revealing a smaller room of wood panels and no windows. The compact table of scented candles also held a small assortment of religious statues of varying faiths, mostly Eastern. Against the far wall was a large, ornate cabinet made of lacquered wood. The light flickered off tendrils of inlaid stone. "I'm not unaccustomed to death, 'Crimson Cutlass,'" she said, lighting a few more candles on sconces. "I simply do not wish to court it any more than I have to. There's enough of it in this city and this age as it is."

"They're criminals," he retorted.

She looked at him, though her smile held some playfulness. "Even men can be redeemed."

Crimson tried not to chuckle. "Yes," he agreed, "yes, they can. But the men who came here tonight – no, not them."

"How do you know about them?" she asked, her voice genuine.

"I've been following their progress ever since they came to Chicago a few months ago." He frowned. "And I'd met them before." He took off one glove and ran his hands down the side of the cabinet. "It's beautiful. Where did you get it?"

"India," Chameleon answered. "It was my father's, a gift from the Maharajah for saving him from the Tiger of Eschnapur."

"It doesn't look Indian."

"No," she agreed. "It's an ancient sarcophagus. No one knows who made it. I found my cloak inside," she paused, "after my father died."

Crimson walked over to her. Their eyes met and he took the edge of her cloak between his bare fingertips. His face moved close to hers. "Yes, your cloak. That's what they came here for tonight."

"Boss?" The voice had come from back inside the living room. It was a young man, worried and moving fast. "Boss?"

The moment was broken, and Crimson turned with a dramatic flair of his greatcoat, exiting the secret room. "Over here, Mikey. I'm alright."

The Chameleon followed him and shut the secret panel. "You brought friends?"

Without looking back he held aloft his wrist, showing the pulsing red of the radio signal imbedded in the fake jewel. "I alerted my man."

"And he can pick locks," she observed.

"It's good to know people with vocational skills."

"Boss," Mikey said, entering from the foyer. The man was in his early forties, a simple wool coat hanging off his somewhat stocky frame. He gestured at the dissipating gas and the mess of bodies. "Wha' happened?" he asked in his cockney accent. He glanced at the masked woman and nodded his drivers cap at her once. "Ma'am."

Crimson's eyes darted to the still-prone figure of the man he had secured. "The Conclave arrived and found the lady of the house out, and that a tigress had taken her place. Mikey, this is the fabled Chameleon of Chicago folklore."

"How do you do?" she greeted him.

"Ma'am," Mikey repeated.

"Do you have the truck this evening?" Crimson asked his trusted valet. When Mikey nodded in the affirmative, he told him, "here are your instructions, then. Take the deceased to the drop point, but on the way, leave the bound survivor on the steps of this address." He handed a slip of paper to Mikey. "He'll be our message to the Conclave: 'Genevieve Donovan is under my protection.' Understood?"

"Aye, cap'n," Mikey answered, and easily shouldered one of the dead assassins, carrying him outside.

Crimson turned to the masked woman. "The conclave aren't petty thugs; they'll try again. You'll want to, uh, disappear for a while."

Chameleon was shaking her head before he had even finished his pun. "Like hell, *monsieur*. We take care of ourselves here." She crossed her arms and leaned against a stately grandfather clock. "I'll dump the carpet, call the cops and tell them I had an attempted break in. They'll lend some protection here for the next few nights while we hunt this Conclave down."

"We?" Crimson echoed with a grin. "Very well, Chameleon, my dear." He took her gloved hand and kissed it, his eyes peering up at hers from above his dark bandana mask. "It's a plan."

He sheathed his sword on its baldric and unholstered his strange pistol, connecting a wire from his belt to a hook he placed in one barrel. "I'll see you tomorrow night, on the roof." There was a loud shot, and the grappler sailed through the broken skylight above.

"Hmm," she fished, "do I trust a masked man who won't divulge his name?"

"Inconsequential," he answered. "You're intrigued." With that he sailed up through the air on the retracting line and was gone.

"Cocky," She said.

Chapter 2

Professor John Clark dove into the small pond behind the mansion on his sprawling grounds. He swam deep, straight towards the bottom. He ignored the encroaching darkness and pressure that engulfed him despite the clear spring water; having made this dive a hundred times before, he could swim it blindfolded. He swam every morning whether he decided to bring anything up from the secreted chest or not. It kept him in peek condition.

When he came up he rested his arms on the small wooden boat waiting for him. The pre-dawn's dim light was caught and reflected in a small ruby he held between two fingers. John showed it to the boat's occupant, a Japanese-American man named Dr. Mifune.

"Have Jerry get that appraised, as usual," John said.

Mifune took the gem and adjusted his glasses. "Yes, that should cover the next range of experiments. Thank you, John."

"My pleasure," he answered and pulled himself out of the water. "This swim always makes me feel like Johnny Weissmuller." He had dark hair, short in back but long enough on top that he had to slick it over. Water ran down his cold skin, glistening off chiseled features. John threw a towel around his broad shoulders.

"You sure you don't mean the Count of Monte Cristo?" Mifune smirked, gesturing to the hidden treasure deep below.

"Hmm?" John began toweling off and laughed. "Oh, yes. I'm certain that's where I got the idea from in the first place."

"Down there," Mifune mused, "is where the Crimson Cutlass keeps his fabled stash of riches, eh?"

John looked at his trusted friend. "Yes, doctor. Well, some of it, anyway. Some I decided to invest, some I suspect is still scattered near Grandfather's ship. What little he took ashore he squandered, and he never had the ability to go back and retrieve the rest."

"So," Mifune changed subjects, "you were saying that the cloak rendered the young lady genuinely invisible?"

"Yes," John nodded, and began rowing them back to the small dock.

"Fascinating," Mifune wondered. "If you were not Professor John Clark as well as the Crimson Cutlass, I might doubt your word, sir."

"I don't blame you."

"How is it possible?"

John thought a moment. "I don't know, though I suspect it has something to do with the ancient sarcophagus she said she found it in."

Mifune pulled a face. "What, *Chandu* and all that silly Indian mysticism? I don't think so."

"Nevertheless, there's something queer about that cabinet, Doctor." John smiled charmingly. "Don't fret – I intend to find out more. How could I possibly pass up such a beautiful and mystifying young lady?"

"Indeed."

~

"Mornin', Boss,"

"Good morning, Mikey," John answered, tipping his fedora with a cane. He faked a slight limp publicly, even in the confines of his own estate's outdoors.

Mikey was polishing the black limousine in the drive out front of the main house. "You need a ride, gov'?"

"Downtown, please." He handed his cane to Mikey and got into the seat behind the driver and waited for him to start the car. "You dropped that Conclave crony at the warehouse I indicated last night?"

"Yes, boss," Mikey said. You don't think that's their headquarters, do you? It seems a bit..."

"Obvious?" John finished. "I agree. No, I think that is a staging area for some of their activity, though. With luck, he'll have been taken back to the headquarters to answer for his failure personally. In which case, by now..." He took a sort of portable radio device from inside his coat and switched it on. A homing signal began warbling quietly coinciding with a flashing red bulb. "We should be able to home in on the signaling device I placed on him."

Mikey smiled. "Another of Doctor Mifune's devices, gov'?"

John tried not to look hurt. "I got it working," he explained. "Mifune simply made it... practical."

"Yeah? How big was it before?" Mikey asked.

"About the size of a cinder block." When Mikey stifled a laugh, John said "Drive."

~

Soon they were within the confines of Chicago's inner city. People were going about their daily business, the men in their suits and hats, the ladies in their skirts. John's limo passed cafes and newsstands, soda fountains and department stores. The homing device beeped along steadily, increasing a bit more as they approached an industrial area not far from Lake Michigan, and picked up an octave when they passed over a steel girder bridge.

"We're getting closer," John mused.

"Aye, cap'n," Mikey answered. "About time, too."

"Make your next left, Mikey," John told his driver. "Flip the license plate and activate the tinting."

Mikey flipped a switch on the polished dashboard and the passenger windows began to darken. "Done," was all he said.

They turned down an alley and were soon pulling alongside a large brick structure.

"Another warehouse," Mikey observed.

"Yes," John agreed, "though I suspect that their base of operations is primarily beneath it. And even then, I doubt Dr. Faustus is within the same building. He's too clever for that." He rubbed his chin absently. "Alright Mikey, drive on. The secrets of the Conclave of Three will keep until tonight, when the Crimson Cutlass at last pays them a visit."

Mikey glanced over his shoulder. "And what of the Chameleon, boss?"

John smiled to himself. "Yes, I think the Chameleon will be there as well."

～

Two henchmen of the Conclave of Three held up their compatriot between them. The third man was the same masked fiend the Crimson Cutlass had left alive the evening before. His hands were still bound behind his back and purple bruising had started to swell on his face. One of the men reached out and flipped a switch on a control box, and a curtain in front of them opened. A second switch was set, and a wall opened to reveal white glass, showing the silhouette of a desk and some sort of technical apparatus. A figure was seated at the desk, tall and imposing, though whether this all was a scene from the next room or some sort of illusion or transmission, none of the henchmen knew. There was a speaker box near the switch.

"Report," came a grave voice from the dark scene beyond.

"This man is the only survivor of the group sent to Genevieve Donovan's home," said the man who had worked the controls. They all had German accents. "He was found bound and barely conscious near warehouse two."

"Explain yourself," the silhouette commanded.

The swaying henchman between them could only stammer. "I - I don't know what happened. I had... I had him...."

"Fool," came the strange voice from beyond. "You were warned of her abilities, and yet you failed me."

The two men holding the henchman forced him to his knees. "There was a note attached to him," said the other, "signed by the Crimson Cutlass."

A sound of frustrated anger seethed from the darkened man. "And you were told that the Crimson Cutlass might know of our activities since we arrived. Your failure is complete."

"No," pleaded the guilty henchman, but he knew it was far too late.

"Destroy him," came the order. "Herr Davidoff shall command the next mission. An agent will arrive later today with further instructions. There will be no further failures."

"Yes, Doctor," the two henchmen answered, bowing low.

"No, no!" the condemned wailed, but he was powerless when the others dragged him to his doom.

~

"A flower shop, boss?" Mikey seemed confused.

"The closest one, please, yes." John hid his expression, but it was Genevieve's face he could not stop thinking about. The young woman was a beauty with a strength that surprised him, and John was rarely surprised. "I want to make certain they're delivered this evening, before the Crimson Cutlass goes hunting tonight."

"So step on it," Mikey said. "I get it."

"And contact Danny Walsh. Tell him to meet us at the house tonight."

"Right, gov'."

The limo pulled up next to a flower stand and John began perusing the selection from his seat. "Yes," he said, opening the door. "This will do."

"Professor John Clark," Mikey said with a raised brow, "courting."

John ignored him, shopping for a bouquet that he thought might go well with those masked eyes. He made his selection and paid, writing down the address it was to be delivered to for the runner. He left a generous tip and got back into his car.

"Mr. Walsh has been alerted," Mikey announced.

"Good," John thanked him. "Head for home."

Chapter 3

Genevieve anxiously looked out the window closest to the door and noticed the cop still standing there. A part of her felt as though she had placed a sign on her door saying that she was, indeed, the Chameleon, and that the threatening mob would find her easily now that her home was under police protection. But she knew that was irrational; the mob she so often thwarted did not know the true identity of the costumed woman they wanted dead. But the Conclave she had met the night before, they knew, and they were coming for her again. The Chameleon could, of course, easily leave whenever she wanted to. But she was waiting – waiting for a man who had promised to show her more of the strange world she was now a part of. His eyes had held hers, letting their guard down just long enough to pull at Genevieve's soul. Yes, she conceded silently, she was intrigued.

"I've checked all the windows, miss," said the pretty, young house servant. Mary Carlisle had been Genevieve's friend and employee ever since she had found her trying to break in three years before. Now the former urchin was dressed as a chauffeur, complete with a cap that matched her black leggings. In contrast, Genevieve was pacing in a long silken gown. "Nothing's been tried, and I couldn't see anything that might have been added. The home is secure, miss."

"Thank you, Mary." Genevieve said.

"A strange turn of events, miss," Mary said. When her mistress raised an eyebrow she continued. "Normally I feel I'd find you investigating the movements and possible connections of Carlucci or somebody's men, even at this time of day. Not pacing like a caged animal. This must be a new threat indeed."

"It is," Genevieve agreed, "and I can see that until I get some answers as to who this Conclave is and how they know my identity, I'm going to feel..." She trailed off, and when Mary's questioning look caught her eye she finished succinctly with "put out". The two young women shared a laugh. "And answers I shall get, from this mysterious Crimson Cutlass. Tonight."

Excited by the subject of the city's other masked vigilante, Mary came closer to her friend and employer. "There's been rumors of him on the streets for years, miss. They say he's the ghost of a pirate hanged for his evil deeds decades ago, and now he hunts murderers and cutthroats at night to repent his wicked past."

Genevieve suppressed a chuckle. "He's real enough. His leg was certainly solid when he used it to trip me last night. Though I'm a bit surprised that I'd seen nothing of him at all in the nights since I arrived in

Chicago. I thought I was the one who was invisible."

Mary shrugged. "You've been busy; distracted, if I may say so, miss. You've been following front page gangsters, not phantom rogues buried on page nine."

Genevieve nodded. "Until now."

"What the...?" Mary had turned to the front window. "Hey!" she yelled at the scene unfolding outside.

There was a sound like a scuffle, then someone being thrown to the ground.

Genevieve's heart jumped to her throat; something was happening out front, and the cop was nowhere to be seen.

Night had fallen, and the Crimson Cutlass observed the rooftops from the shadows. Cool air wafted between Chicago's high rises from the lake, taking the smoke from Genevieve Donovan's penthouse chimney and passing it hazily over her skylight, already repaired. He had been watching the area for some time from his hiding place and had seen no movement, friend or foe. He had hoped to catch a glimpse of her, perhaps coming outside to wait for him. He shook the thought off and decided that now was as good a time as any to get reacquainted.

Crimson hooked a line to the tiny winch hidden within one of the leather pouches on his belt. Using it to slow his descent, he swung out from the building he had been waiting on and glided down to land on the Donovan rooftop. With a practiced flourish, he unhooked the line and moved stealthily across the rooftop to the skylight.

Crimson froze.

"Looking for a peepshow?" The voice was disembodied, coming from somewhere in the darkness nearby, but it was definitely Genevieve. "I'm afraid I've already changed."

He looked in the general direction of her voice in time to see her shapely leg materialize out of thin air, as if an invisible curtain had been pulled aside. Crimson's breath stopped in his chest at the sight of the Chameleon. He couldn't tear his eyes from her - beautiful, vulnerable and strong all at once. She smiled slightly from beneath her hood, seeming to almost laugh at her own joke, and the scene made his heart skip a beat. Her full-length cloak shimmered from formless to black cloth as she tossed it over her shoulder and stood proudly, coiling her bullwhip between her gloved hands. The stocking clad leg was shown well from a high-slit up one side of her gown. She was in the same corset and mask as the night before, now fully in her element.

He tried not to shake himself from his reverie too obviously. "You look fantastic," was all he could say.

Chameleon paused, possibly deciding how to take that. She laughed the compliment away finally, though there was a hint of self-consciousness in her body language. "Rogue," she said.

He grinned. "Did you get the flowers?"

The Chameleon's eyes flashed heavenward. "That *was* you." She was annoyed. "I didn't know if that was you, some admirer, the mob or the Conclave that sent those, but either way the cop almost killed that poor boy when he tried to deliver them. I hope you tipped him well."

Crimson blanched inwardly. "I did." He changed the subject. "Did you have any other visitors today?"

"Just the repairmen," she said, nodding at the roof. "Who is this Conclave of the Three? What do they want? I understand this cloak is unique, but what do they want it for?"

"That's precisely what I've been trying to find out." He tipped his hat and bowed. "Shall we go inside, discuss things further?"

"I thought we were going hunting for them before they come back for 'Genevieve Donovan?'"

"We are," Crimson agreed, "But I want another look at that cloak of yours and the cabinet it came in. Meanwhile, I'll tell you some of what I know of the Conclave."

The Chameleon let her breath out. "Okay, but ignore the mess." She began to lead him inside.

"Mess - what did you do all day?" he asked quietly.

The Chameleon turned and glared.

~

Back inside the secret sanctum within Genevieve's apartments, The Chameleon was lighting candles again. "I can't believe I brought you in here last night," she murmured. "I never even take Mary in here, and I've known her three years."

"Your servant," he guessed. "Where is she?"

"Watching the house. She's very adept at moving quietly. I caught her trying to rob me when I first met her."

"So naturally you made her your trusted servant," Crimson said.

"Naturally." She removed her opera gloves and took off her cloak, draping it over one arm. Chameleon ran her bare fingertips along the polished wood of the cabinet, down to the bands of metal and gemstone that decorated its exterior near one of the clasps. "The cabinet was given to my father in India as a gift," she said. "I'll never know if he ever opened it or knew the properties of this cloak within. But I imagine that the Maharajah gave it to him in the hopes that he would use it to help others." She smiled, thinking of the past. "We were... an adventurous family. I'd seen a third of the world before I was sixteen, it seems. Daddy was vigorous and good hearted."

She opened the sarcophagus and hung the cloak on the standing wooden dais there. Crimson noticed a sort of phosphorescence faintly emanating from within. Chameleon then picked up her candle and stepped aside, lighting the interior of the cabinet for the Crimson Cutlass to see.

The reflection was almost blinding. The entire interior of the cabinet was inlaid with rivulets of strange metals or veins of precious minerals. Quartz, mother-of-pearl, gemstone, and a myriad of others, all smooth to the touch and somehow perfectly laid out in a design that covered the whole of its insides. It was like an impossible painting made by a brush textured by a rock collector's dreams.

"My God," he said. "It's incredible."

"There's strata in there I've never seen in all my travels," Chameleon told him. "I've discreetly asked masons, collectors, dealers, miners, and checked books – I'm convinced that at least some of the stones used to make this can't be found anywhere else on Earth. It's as though this thing fell from the sky and someone encased it in lacquered wood."

Crimson rolled back on his boot heels. "Or someone found a piece of another world and used it to make this cabinet," he surmised.

"Yes," she agreed. "Whatever it is, it gives the cloak its power."

Crimson felt the material between his fingertips yet again, running the velvety black cloth over his skin. If the cloak was as old as the cabinet may be, then it was just as impossible, for it was still in almost perfect condition. "How do you know?"

"Because if I leave it out too long, its ability to blend or turn invisible diminishes."

He studied her. "Amazing. The cloak's properties allow it to soak up something within the cabinet that has the power to make it invisible. How do you control it?"

"Force of will," she said simply. "When I put it on it naturally wants to blend with its surroundings, but if I think hard enough I simply vanish, or relax completely and then it becomes a black cloak."

Crimson was amazed. "Its little wonder someone should come looking for this if they heard there was a person with the power to become invisible running around Chicago. You could assassinate anyone with this cloak. Go anywhere, hear anything."

The Chameleon raised an eyebrow. "You don't think that's a bit thin? The Conclave of Three came here just based on rumors, somehow managed to track me here to try and steal it?"

Crimson put his gloves back on. "It's one of a couple theories at the moment," he told her. "More likely it's a combination of things; I believe our enemy had already heard of the cloak and tracked it to you in the long run. Dr. Faustus has agents everywhere – his influence stretches very far, which isn't hard to understand when you know some of his colleagues and network."

"Dr. Faustus?" Chameleon asked. "The leader of the Conclave of the Three, I suppose?"

Crimson nodded solemnly. "Put your cloak on – I'll tell you more on the way. It's time we found just where Dr. Faustus is hiding himself in this city. Maybe then we can unravel just how he came to know of your skill."

~

The Chameleon followed Crimson Cutlass out of her secret room. "This way," she said, indicating a hall leading back upstairs.

"No, this way," he told her and gestured towards the front of the house.

"I thought we were taking the rooftops," she replied, confused. "What about the beat cops or any thugs?"

Crimson laughed, but it was charming. "I have a car waiting. We tracked the Conclave to a warehouse this afternoon. But you're right; we can't very well be seen leaving out the front, can we? Perhaps I'm distracted," he added, his eyes briefly passing over her.

"It might be a bit obvious," Chameleon raised an eyebrow. "Leaving that way. I have my own exits."

"Lead on."

He gestured to the flowers he'd sent sitting in a vase. "So you at least kept them?" Crimson asked incredulously.

She turned and patted his cheek through the bandana. In retrospect, she found the sudden motion intimate and somehow comfortable. "I couldn't throw them out after all the trouble that poor delivery boy went through, now could I?"

She led him to a side entrance and checked the alley up and down before leading the way. Out front, Chameleon was surprised to find Mary talking to the driver of a large black car with darkened windows. The man in the driver's cap was Mikey, Crimson's valet. Both servants were suddenly quiet and attentive the moment Mary spotted their approaching masters.

Mary cleared her throat. "Begging your pardon, miss. I'll get the door for you."

"Yes," Crimson said flatly, "nothing obvious about any of this." He glanced at his valet.

"Sorry, sir." Mikey looked sheepishly at the pretty servant then to his master before ducking into the driver seat. "Where to, boss?"

The Crimson Cutlass settled into the dark back seat beside the Chameleon. "Warehouse 'A'."

"Aye, cap'n." The car began its journey.

The Chameleon crossed her legs. "So, tell me about Dr. Faustus."

"Herr Doktor Faustus," he nodded. "He is the mystery I have been trying to unravel for some time now. Research has been difficult, but I believe he was a lieutenant of Dr. Mabuse before coming to work for Der Fuhrer himself."

"Mabuse?"

"A hypnotist and gambler who killed from the shadows and targeted Germany's elite. He disappeared around the time that Hitler came to power. But Faustus is not a known member of the Nazi Party, and none of his thugs bear standard German emblems. I suspect he's part of some other faction."

"Wait, slow down," the Chameleon demanded. "The Nazis are after my cloak?"

"No, not Hitler," Crimson corrected. "A criminal mastermind, Dr. Faustus has an influence in Nazi politics, a private army of mercenaries, and a history buried deep in myth and rumors. His operation has some technology the likes of which I've never seen before. Since I accidentally crossed paths with his men a year ago in New York, I've been working to find out more about him."

"Where have I heard his name before?" She asked.

"German folklore. Faust made a pact with the devil; his soul in exchange for power over life and death. The story is hundreds of years old, and in some versions the name was originally Faustus."

The Chameleon raised an eyebrow. "So he claims immortality?"

Crimson shrugged. "Whoever he was before his involvement with the criminal underworld in the 1920s, I haven't been able to trace him." He watched the rooftops through the windows of the car, studying their surroundings as well as watching for danger. After a moment he said, "Faustus learned his craft well; I've barely been able to track his movements, much less discover anything about his past. No one has ever even actually seen him. Perhaps not even Adolf."

"He gives me the willies already." Chameleon absently rubbed her arms through the opera gloves. She glanced at the Crimson Cutlass when she realized that now he was studying her. "Don't worry," she said defensively and looked away. "I'm up for this. No fascist stooge and his band of cronies is going to get the better of me, sir."

She could hear the smile in his reply. "I know. No, actually I was just thinking how attractive and strong I find you, not the opposite. You're certainly not like most women."

She shrugged. "Most haven't been where I have."

"True."

The car slowed. "We're coming up on the warehouse, cap'n," Mike said.

"Drop us here," Crimson told him. "If we need anything or if you have to move..."

"Got it," Mike said, and held up wrist communicator. "I'll be monitoring, sir."

Crimson Cutlass and the Chameleon got out of the large black car and began ascending the rungs of a ladder leading to the rooftops of an adjoining warehouse, with Crimson leading.

He paused, looking down at her. "Who's guarding your place?"

"Mary," she replied obviously. "I sent the cop home in case things got..." She tugged at her cloak and mask for emphasis, saying only, "weird". They began climbing again. "Any idea how this Dr. Faustus found me?"

"Yes," Crimson told her, "but you won't like it."

They reached the roof and tread carefully.

"You might as well tell me." Chameleon put the hood of her cloak up, ready at a moment's notice to make her form invisible. She paused, and a thought seemed to come to her. "The Maharajah?"

"Dead," Crimson confirmed. "I'm sorry. His daughters were taken by Faustus' men and sold to the highest bidder. That was how this all started for me; tracking them."

"His daughters!" she exclaimed.

But Crimson shushed her, holding up a gloved hand.

The Chameleon wrapped her cloak about her and was gone. Invisible to the naked eye, she moved forward beside her new comrade, watching the shadows around them.

"There," he pointed. "That's the warehouse we tracked your attacker to after his colleagues found him."

"What's the plan?" she whispered.

"Sneak inside, see what we can find out," he answered simply. "With luck things will get... interesting."

"With luck?!"

He smirked in the direction of her voice. "Where's your sense of adventure?"

Chapter 4

The curtains parted, and a black clad henchman of Dr. Faustus bowed before the silhouette of his master. "The agents have been sent as you ordered, Herr Doktor. I expect word soon."

"Herr Davidov is leading them?" the strange voice from beyond asked.

"He personally took charge of the operation," the henchman said with a curt nod, though he could only assume that his mysterious leader could see it. "He is with them now."

"Very well. Here are your instructions."

The man clicked his heels and attentively listened.

The curtain closed of its own accord.

～

The Crimson Cutlass removed a wire and small grappling hook from a pouch along one belt. He twirled it like a lasso, snagging a fire escape railing along the opposite side of the street's rooftop. "Have you ever done this?" he asked, holding out the line towards where he thought she was standing.

"Brought my own, thanks," the Chameleon replied. Her arms appeared from the thin air her cloak reflected, and she snapped her whip towards the same point as the grappler. The cloak fluttered aside when she tipped over the edge and swung across to the warehouse.

"Atta girl," Crimson smiled. He followed her over, his own black coat billowing in the wind.

Upon the roof of the enemy headquarters the pair moved quickly but quietly. The Chameleon's movements were all but completely invisible, and her dainty steps were stealthy yet sure-footed. Crimson smiled, reflecting on how the girl constantly surprised him.

"I'd like to think we'll get lucky and find Faustus himself here tonight. They say he's a beastly thing to behold."

Chameleon tutted. "Hearsay." Her arms appeared briefly from beneath the invisible cloak as she made a show of adjusting her opera gloves. "Have you seen any real sign of this Faustus?"

Crimson threw a mischievous smile her way. "No one has. But I have reason to believe he's right here in Chicago, personally making certain that whatever devious machinations he's devising are seen through to fruition. And that includes the theft of your cloak."

"He'll not have it," she responded with resolution.

"Because we're going to stop him," Crimson agreed.

He reached the door first and put his ear to it momentarily before working at the lock with a pick.

"You're pretty quiet with that thing," Chameleon whispered. She sounded impressed.

"A guard will be close," he said. The lock clicked, and he gave her the okay sign, hoping she had seen him. "Right, here we go." He opened the door and slipped in to the building. Crimson saw only the briefest flash of the Chameleon's knee and boot as her invisible cloak brushed past him. He closed the door and made his way down the stairs.

Chameleon's voice was the only thing in the hallway. "Where to next?"

"Let's see where this leads," he answered.

The next door led to a choice of three more darkened halls. "Do you want to split up?" She asked.

"If you like," Crimson replied. "I expected to find a warehouse, instead we see a series of empty hallways. Let's meet back here in twenty minutes. If things get rough, I'll see you at the car."

"Agreed."

⁂

The Chameleon kept her cloak wrapped around her and ran into the darkness. The hall curved away to the right and she found a set of doors, so she chose one and gave a listen before trying the knob. It wasn't locked, and she quietly entered.

The room was unoccupied and empty except for a few small, open crates of wood with German markings. *At least we're on the right track*, Chameleon thought, and swept out of the room.

The next door was locked, so Chameleon produced her set of ancient and modern lock picks from the tiny bag on her hip and knelt down. She made quick work of the lock and peeked through the crack in the door. The room beyond was filled with racks of rifles and handguns, with some of the slots empty, which she took to mean there were armed guards in the building.

Chameleon pulled the door closed and froze just before the lock could catch; a uniformed and armed member of the Conclave of Three had turned down the hallway and was heading right for her. The guard stopped in his tracks, the strange, masked visage cocking to one side like an attentive dog. Chameleon followed his perceived gaze and swore under her breath when she realized that her boot's toe was showing in the dim light, having slipped out from beneath her invisible cloak. She stood up, letting the gathered material unfurl and slide back over her foot, returning her to complete stealth and letting the guard ponder what she hoped he might take as a trick of the light. The Chameleon brought her fists up into a stance, watching the Conclave guard inch uncertainly towards her.

The guard's head turned to watch the door open of its own accord, Chameleon's toe having tapped the base of the door. She used the distraction to leap forward and strike; her fist slammed into the man's chin, knocking his head back and expelling a surprised cry from his lungs. Using the butt of her whip's handle like a blackjack, Chameleon cracked the guard's skull, rendering him unconscious. Satisfied, she stepped back - directly into the arms of the second guard that had snuck up behind her. She barely managed to call out before a gloved hand clasped over her mouth and darkness took her.

༺༻

Crimson had finally found an open portion of the warehouse, and it was a doozey. A huge hanger and storage area opened before him, with a large stretch of it closest to the hanger doors submerged and leading out into Lake Michigan.

Crimson hid silently until some of the Conclave soldiers had left the area. The two armed men had been moving crates onto decking that led to huge flying boat docked within the hanger next to a few small boats. He checked his watch, deciding that he had time to investigate. He ran down to the plane.

It was a full-sized aircraft of possibly European origins resembling a Dornier Do24, able to take at least thirty people or a large cargo a fair distance, but he'd never seen one quite like it. He found a manifest pinned to one of the crates; the plane was bound for someplace called Togabiza. He noticed a copy of the same document stapled to another of the boxes and tore it free, stuffing it in his pocket. Near the crates were piles of cable and chain and a large winch. All of it seemed bound for the Conclave's mysterious next destination.

A door squealed as it was pulled open by the Conclave guards. Crimson moved like a quick shadow, first ducking behind the crates, then moving through the semi-darkness towards the wall. He let the armed men pass where he had been investigating, then slipped out the door.

In the hall, Crimson checked his watch.

༺༻

Cold air on bare skin and biting metal bonds were the Chameleon's first waking sensations. The handcuffs secured her wrists behind her to a metal chair, and her vision was blindfolded. Her cloak and opera gloves had been removed, and a strap of her gown had slipped off one shoulder. A moan escaped her parted lips unbidden.

Panic threatened to overwhelm her, but the Chameleon had been in tough scrapes before. Her legs were bound at the ankles but otherwise free. She straightened in her chair despite the protest of sore muscles and controlled her breathing, letting her senses stretch out. Her hearing and a taste of atmosphere told her that the room wasn't large, and she was fairly certain that at least one other person was in the room with her. She cursed inwardly when she remembered that some of her lock picks were secreted in her gloves, but she began fumbling with the cuffs anyway with her bare fingertips. They weren't standard handcuffs, that much she could tell. Crimson had said that Dr. Faustus and at least some of his men were German. She hoped that her new friend was on his way.

"She's awake."

A gruff hand yanked her head back by her hair and she cried out and cursed the man with language fouler than she normally cared to utter. The hand held tight to her regardless. The voice connected to it had sounded German.

A light came on somewhere in front of the Chameleon, as though a window shade had been opened on a large window. She could barely see beneath her blindfold, but she knew that it was artificial light.

"Good." The answering voice was sinister and grave, though it sounded as though it had come from a speaker. "Chameleon," the voice addressed her, "or as the social norm of Chicago knows you, Genevieve Donovan. Just another rich socialite, but with one gift – a cloak from an ancient cabinet with fantastical properties. Tell us about it."

"Dr. Faustus, I presume," she answered, then told him where they could all go.

She nearly got whiplash from how fast her hair was pulled back. "Dr. Faustus asked you a question, *frauline* – you answer."

The speaker voice chuckled. "If there is indeed a fiery pit, dear girl, believe me - you'll be there long before I."

Chameleon's head was yanked again, causing her to arch her back and grit her teeth. "The cloak is a family heirloom, you mad bastard – that's all I know." She howled when the fingers in her dark locks twisted. "You Germans like it rough, eh?" But tears were threatening to spill over onto her cheeks. "Tell me, Herr Doktor – do you really think you're immortal?"

"She plays for time, *mein Doktor.*"

"Show us the cloak," Dr. Faustus voice instructed. Blessedly the hand released Chameleon. *Us*, he had said. "Put it on."

She heard her cloak rustle as the man beside her flung the long garment around his shoulders and fixed the clasp.

"*Mein Gott*," Faustus' voice said in amazement. "It works perfectly. Already his form dissipates."

"I'm glad you're impressed," she said dryly. "I've already used to beat several of your men into unconsciousness."

"Remove the cloak," Dr. Faustus commanded. "Place it on the table."

There was a new voice from the speaker. "Show us the girl," it growled.

Chameleon froze, and a new fear the likes of which she had never encountered crept into her soul. The voice had been both deep and high-pitched, with a gurgling unease as if a forked tongue were rolling around in a mouth that didn't quite know English. Something about it was demonic and sinister, and not just the notion of what its speaker intended. Chameleon was convinced that it was not human.

"*Mein Herr?*"

"You heard the Masters of the Conclave of Three," Faustus' voice ordered. "Remove the prisoner's garments."

The pig beside her laughed under his breath and moved to stand in front of her. Her sight was still denied, making the sense of his closeness and heat of his hands all the more menacing. His breath moved close to her ear.

"No," she involuntarily whispered.

His ungloved fingers found the slit of her dress and tossed it aside revealing the tops of her stocking-clad thighs. Chameleon's shoulders hunched reflexively at his touch, and she began to struggle in her bonds.

"You see, Ms. Donovan," Faustus began to explain, "The Masters have been cultivating a certain adoration for the flesh of females."

The guard grasped the laces at the front of her corset and pulled violently, causing Chameleon to jerk in her chair. She heard the pop of strings and seams as the garment was rent open. He paused briefly to huff triumphantly against her ear.

Faustus dolled on. "They prefer mating with the more comely examples of our species, so naturally they wish to see your worthiness. You understand."

When she tried to pull away or tip her seat, the guard grabbed her by the hair again. He stepped aside so that his masters could see his handiwork, then hooked the front of her dress with his free hand and tore it open, revealing the pink satin of her brassier. He began to pull the dress down her shoulders, but found he needed to pull the damaged corset wider.

"More," came the beastly other voice again. "She is a perfect specimen.

More."

The guard pawed at Chameleon's gown, tearing the slit wide open up to the base of her corset, revealing her panties and garters. At last she screamed.

Chapter 5

There was a smash behind her, and Chameleon heard the kicked-open door slam against the wall. There was a click of a cocking mechanism and she flinched when the following shot deafened the chamber. Through the ringing in her ears she heard a breath escape the guard when he was struck and felt a spray of his blood. He thudded to the ground near her feet.

Two more shots rang out and the lit screen in front of Chameleon shattered and went dark. There was a hissing, gurgling sound, but whether it was from the thing who's voice she'd heard or the smashing of glass and sparking of electricity, she could not be sure. Then she felt a warm hand on her shoulder and the heard the clinking of a set of keys picked up from a metal table.

"Are you alright?" It was the Crimson Cutlass. He sounded distressed. Her blindfold slid free and he knelt down to open her cuffs.

"Yes, thanks to you." She sounded genuinely relieved.

Chameleon rubbed her wrists and looked at her rescuer's handiwork. The guard lay dead from a single shot to his chest of Crimson's Gatling-like handgun. She saw that the area in front of her had been some sort of electrical screen; the still-glowing, ruptured tubes of the television and speaker system were all that was left of her tormentor's masters. "I'm sorry they weren't here to have felt those bullets themselves," she said, surprised at the venom in her own voice. "Did you see them?"

"Only silhouettes," Crimson said, handing Chameleon her cloak. "I assume one was Faustus, so what the hell was that next to him?"

She wrapped the cloak over her torn clothes and bared body. "I was hoping you could..." Chameleon snatched her bullwhip from the table and it snaked out in an instant, snapping in the face of the next guard who came running into the room. It sliced open the man's face up to his eye-mask and he fell aside, screaming.

Crimson's gun raised and fired a hail of bullets, tearing into the next two men to race in with their own guns. He aimed again and finished off the man Chameleon had felled. "We need to get out of here."

And alarm began to sound throughout the building.

"I agree," she said.

The duo ran out of the room and headed down a flight of stairs. She followed him into another room within the warehouse. "This way," he said. "I found a window in the office front – we can get out that way."

"So resourceful," she smiled. She didn't know why, but suddenly Chameleon realized that she was having fun. Inwardly she blamed it on the adrenaline. "We must stop rescuing each other like this; people will talk."

The multiple spinning barrels of Crimson's gun made short work of the window. He checked once that the coast was clear outside, then motioned for her to go first. "Let 'em eat cake."

Chameleon dove out the shattered portal. She wrapped her invisibility around her and the pair headed for the car – already Mikey had turned a corner and was heading towards them.

"What if Faustus was somewhere else in the building?" she asked as they got into the car.

"I sincerely hope he was," Crimson answered, and pressed the button on a remote device in his hand.

The warehouse they had just escaped exploded.

～

Crimson pulled at the bandana covering his face and let out a breath with a grin. He had almost forgotten for an instant that the young woman was beside him until her face became visible. Then he reminded himself that there were no such things as accidents. John Clark smiled at Genevieve Donovan.

"Hello," she said.

"Hello."

She seemed to approve of his revealed visage; it was then that she cupped his cheek in her hand and kissed him for the first time.

He kissed her back passionately, pulling her further into his arms. "Genevieve." Their cheeks brushed together and they held tight, both overcome with emotions. "Genevieve, are you alright, darling?"

"I am now." She began laughing and he pulled back to look into her dark eyes. When his expression became quizzical, she said, "I don't even know your real name!"

Crimson laughed and said, "John. Professor John Clark."

"Professor?" She smiled whimsically. "I've heard your name mentioned at certain social functions. I'm amazed we had never met before."

"It only took masked vigilantism to bring us together, darling." They nuzzled each other quietly for a moment longer.

Mikey looked over his shoulder from the driver's seat. "Where we headed, boss?"

"We should head back to Genevieve's penthouse, make certain that everything there is alright," John said.

"I agree," Genevieve said and gave John a nudge. "That is, if Mikey remembers the way back to Mary's boss's place."

"Of all the cheek," Mikey droned.

～

The front door was broken open and there was a dead cop in the bushes.

Genevieve was out of the car and headed for the busted egress before Mikey had finished pulling up. She called out for Mary, though she donned the hood of her cloak as the Chameleon, masking her approach. The Crimson Cutlass trailed close behind her, his weapons raised.

"Mary?" she said again and pushed past the broken door.

Crimson stopped only to make certain the policeman's bullet wounds were indeed fatal. "Chameleon, wait," he cried. It suddenly seemed an odd thing, trying to balance a newfound romance with staying in character. He worried just as much what they might find as what might still be waiting for them. "Mikey, check the perimeter," he ordered as the valet trailed from the street. "Hit your sonic alarm if you find anything."

Crimson had only just stepped into Genevieve's rooms when a body crashed to the floor at his feet. The prone figure, his neck having snapped upon impact, was a member of the Conclave. Crimson looked up in time to see the Chameleon materialize when she removed her hood and looked down from the banister. "Nice throw," he told her. "An assassin left behind by the Conclave; there may be more."

"So be careful," she told him. She donned her invisibility again.

"That's what I was gonna say," Crimson muttered.

A cursory examination of the penthouse revealed no further bodies, friend or foe, but the wall hiding the secret chamber of the cabinet had been torn out. Entering the room, Crimson found it empty aside from debris and an obviously shocked Genevieve. Visibly distraught, she turned and buried her face in John's embrace. "They've taken my cabinet," she wept. Before he could reply, she pulled away, rushing back into the main rooms of her home. "Mary!" she cried again, desperate to find her friend. "Where is she?"

Mikey walked into the room, shaking his head. "Nothing else out side. No sign of the girl?"

Crimson's shoulders drooped. "She's not here, so we can take comfort hoping she's unharmed. But we have to consider the possibility that she's been taken."

"Taken where?" Genevieve sobbed. She turned away, trying to control her voice. Bracing herself again a wall she shook off her despair. "We destroyed the Conclave's lair. Where would they go?"

Crimson pulled the stolen manifest from his coat. "Here, wherever this may be." He laid the paper out for the others to see. "They had at least one plane ready to go there, and a setup to move large, heavy objects into the cargo hold."

"Looks like it's somewhere in the South Pacific," Mikey noted.

Crimson nodded. "A small island called Togabiza."

~

John made the most of the following days; while he and Genevieve waited for their flight aboard the clipper that would take them to Hawaii, his evenings were spent as the Crimson Cutlass, making certain that the Conclave had indeed fled Chicago for their South Seas destination.

Genevieve was staying within a wing at John's mansion, unable to join him during his nocturnal excursions. "We'll need my cloak when we reach Togabiza," she had explained, placing her miraculous garment in a dark suitcase. "Even now it's powers are fading without the cabinet to recharge them." She did her best to keep busy and do her own research into the Conclave's Chicago holdings, just to be doubly satisfied that they might not be holding her beloved friend Mary someplace close by. She turned and fell into his arms for a moment. She peered up into John's eyes and touched his cheek. "It's maddening, not being able to do more."

John nodded. "I want you with me, darling. It was exciting, having the Chameleon out there by Crimson Cutlass's side." He held up their tickets for the Hawaiian clipper. "And it will be exciting again; Here's our tickets for Honolulu. We leave tomorrow."

Genevieve sat, running her fingers through her hair in exasperation. "We'll get Mary back, won't we?" She gripped his fingers in earnest. "You had said you got the Maharajah's daughters back from those bastards."

"Yes, darling," he said and squeezed her hand. "Everything will work out." He fought hard not to mention the shocking details of the two girls' ordeal or how close a call their eventual rescue was. He wanted desperately for Genevieve to hold on to her hope. But each passing minute made the likelihood of success seem that much more dim.

Chapter 6

The morning of their flight Genevieve awoke from a restless sleep in the settee in her own posh room. She had been tossing and turning in the bed for hours and ended up on the small couch out of frustration. Her rest had been inconstant for days, as much out of worry for Mary as it was for John's nightly missions. She found herself wanting to be close to him, to forget everything and just drop the pretenses and curl up in his arms. Such ideas were pushed aside by her own desires to set things right and find her friend. She started awake and stretched, attempting to work the kink out of her neck.

Still clad in her evening gown, she opened the curtains and saw a small boat out on the lake behind the house in the early morning light. There were two figures in the boat, and when one stood she was certain it was John. She watched him dive into the lake and disappear. Genevieve's curiosity was piqued.

Barefoot, she walked the length of the wooden deck to the edge of the lake and removed her gown. Deciding against too much scandal, she left on the silk pajamas John had provided and dove into the water, swimming out to the boat. By the time she reached the craft and found a smiling Dr. Mifune, John had come up for air.

"Good morning," John said with a smile. He handed something to Dr. Mifune. "I should have known you would be a strong swimmer."

Genevieve shrugged. "I didn't know where any ladies of the house might keep the swimwear."

John raised an eyebrow and regarded her a moment. "Come on down. You showed me your secret room in your place the other night - it's only fitting I show you a secret too." He reached for her hand.

She took it, and together they swallowed air and dove down.

The water was clear and pure, but the light weaker as they swam lower. Even then she could see him finally reach what appeared to be a green and black tarp near the bottom. Pulling it aside, he revealed to her an old wooden chest with metal hinges. He opened it briefly, just long enough to show her the riches inside. The Crimson Cutlass had his own pirate chest beneath the water.

Back at the surface, Genevieve gasped and shook the water away. "You *are* a rogue, indeed, sir!" she said with a laugh.

"What have you two been doing down there?" Dr. Mifune winked.

"Don't let him tease you," John said. "He knows full well what's down there. Dr. Mifune's experiments are for the good of mankind, we hope. But science, as it turns out, is expensive."

"Where did it come from?" Genevieve followed John's lead and they both climbed into the boat, Mifune handing them towels. "Pirate treasure?" she joked.

"Yes," John said resolutely.

"Really?"

"My great-grandfather was a pirate, and his ship sank off the east coast in a squall. Honestly. He squandered what little he managed to come ashore with but settled on the mainland and wrote detailed notes as to where his vessel had gone down. Fortunately for me, my father was an astute historian as well as a decent businessman. I took it upon myself to find a way with today's means to dive down and retrieve what I could at last. I came up with more than you see here. I just keep this as a private stash, as it were - it worked for over a hundred years, might as well take a lesson in keeping my family's fortune safe."

Genevieve laughed. "Amazing. And you thought, 'I'll use it to become a masked pirate against injustice'?"

"And you thought, 'I'll use the family's invisibility cloak and my inheritance to fight mob bosses'?"

Genevieve enjoyed his repost. "You're right, we both sound ridiculous."

"I wouldn't have it any other way."

She studied him. "Who *are* you? Why haven't we met before?"

John smiled and kissed her. It seemed like the first time in ages.

~

The loud hum of the clipper's prop engines permeated the otherwise well-appointed cabin. The craft had been airborne for several hours, and John and Genevieve - still fresh in their romantic mood since the morning's jibes - both awoke from leaning on each other. The plane had been jostled by turbulence.

It seemed like the first sleep either had time for in days. Genevieve stretched. "Why?" She asked suddenly. "What could they possibly want with my cabinet that means taking it to a South Seas island?"

"I wish I knew," John admitted. "I've never come across them having any sort of stronghold or ties to any place even remotely close."

"The Japanese?" she wondered aloud. "Perhaps an alliance?"

"Who knows?" He looked out over the expanse of ocean beneath them from their private passenger compartment. "Maybe it has something to do with that hulking thing hiding with Faustus."

Genevieve turned to him, gripping his arm. "Yes! There was

something... inhuman then, wasn't there? Not only its voice..."

"Something disturbing," John agreed. "Of that there was no doubt. As I said, I only glanced silhouettes, but the figure next to Faustus was... giant and grotesque."

Genevieve laid her head on John's shoulder. "And they've got Mary."

"I know. I'm sorry, I shouldn't have said anything, darling."

She straightened up. "No, best to be as prepared as possible for whatever we face, John - I shan't wilt, I promise."

John caressed her cheek. "You're a standup girl, Ms. Donovan. I'm glad I met you."

Genevieve nodded. She leaned in to kiss him, then pressed her cheek against his. "How much longer before we reach Pearl Harbor?" she asked.

John glanced at his watch. "Several hours. Why?"

Genevieve didn't answer. She got up from the couch in their compartment and pulled closed the door. When next she looked him in the eye, she had already let her dress slip from her shoulders and fall, revealing her stockings and garters beneath her slip. She then hooked the tiny, silk straps of that with her thumbs, letting the garment join the rest at her heels.

John was in her arms in a moment, pressing hot kisses on her lips and neck.

Intermezzo
The Daughters of the Maharajah

It had been as much a stroke of luck as charm, money or prestige might have carried him, but Professor John Clark was in.

The party was as regal – and as private – as anything he had ever heard of going down in New York City, though there were only men among the throng. Everyone was dressed to the nines; the whole scene looked like a J.C. Leyendecker illustration from the *Saturday Evening Post*. Depression of 1937 or not, there was still plenty of money amongst the power-elite. Despite the fact that every man in the dimly lit room wore a masquerade disguise to cover his face, John knew exactly the caliber of those tuxedoed 'gentlemen' in attendance, and someone, somewhere amongst them was Dr. Faustus.

John felt certain that the German mastermind was there, for the elusive enigma himself had organized the secret soiree. He had also been behind the crash of a DC-9 plane, resulting in the death of one of the Crimson Cutlass's agents. Since that event, John and his alter ego had been waiting for an opportunity to strike back, but the good Herr Doktor was so rarely in the U.S., much less notably anywhere except, presumably, Germany. Even that assumption was a guess most of the time. A chance meeting and a promising lead that had uttered Faustus's name had renewed the chase and brought John to New York City. The evening's event was a despicable place to find oneself, but the Crimson Cutlass would remedy that.

The ballroom's lights dimmed.

"Gentlemen," said one man turning to face the rest. "Please, take your seats."

A group of tall, wingback chairs had been arranged in a semi-circle beneath a glass chandelier. John almost forgot to feign his limp when he strode forward a few paces towards the scene.

Six lithe figures in hooded robes entered the room and were led onto a black stage set beneath the glass fixture. The robes were dark, though the material thin – it was obvious now where the females of the party were.

"Bidding will now commence."

Most of the men came forward and sat in the leather seats provided, but John and a few stragglers chose to watch from outside of the circle, each of them with their bidding cards in hand. John was glad of those who chose to stand away like him, hoping it would make it easier for him to slip away soon and don his mask and great coat.

"Thank you." The M.C.'s dialect was an implacable accent from perhaps Eastern Europe. The other men closest to the stage that seemed to be assisting or overseeing the event were dressed similarly to everyone else's tails and masks. John wondered if his quarry were among those assembled closest to the black stage.

"I realize that most of you were drawn here by the evening's main offering," the M.C. began. "However, that sale will be in tandem only, and saved for last. Thus, may I also recommend enjoying bidding on tonight's other items." He motioned to the stage and a bruiser that had been squeezed into a tux led the first robed figure to the forefront of the dais. His meaty hands were easily twice the size of an ordinary man's, yet with careful precision he stopped the figure and slipped the hood and robe from her shoulders. The garment fell away, revealing a young woman, barely more than a girl.

John's breath caught in his throat.

She was as naked as the day she was born, with a foam of golden curls falling down around her sullen, pouty features. Her hands were bound by a tiny silver chain that was held between the fingers of the ape that displayed her.

"Shall we start the bidding at fifteen?"

John had seen enough. Faustus or no, this had to be stopped.

He stepped backwards a few paces, and once he had judged he was far enough out of the light to turn and stride unnoticed, he did so. He walked as quietly as he could, the thick rubber soles of his shoes muffling some of the sound. John turned and hid behind an ornate, Egyptian-themed screen that he had placed his bag near when he had entered. He began rolling up his pant legs.

John pulled the neck of his costumed shoes up and tucked his pant legs into the cavalier boots the shoes transformed into, then exchanged one masquerade for another, donning the uniform of the Crimson Cutlass.

He had been unable to hide his blade amongst the baggage he had waltzed in with, so the Crimson's pistol and a long dagger hidden within his cane would have to do. These he produced once he had completed donning his attire, mask and hat. Properly he could now face the men of this room as his form of masked justice. He cocked the barrel of his gun into place and waited for his moment to reveal himself.

Meanwhile, each of four girls was being sold to the highest bidder for her young flesh. Once sold, she was escorted aside and held in chains, awaiting the ending to the evening's proceedings.

Crimson watched as at last the two main girls were brought forward and shown off to their prospective new masters.

"Our main course of this evening's event, gentlemen," The M.C. announced.

Their coverings were pulled away, revealing two girls of Indian heritage wearing little more than silk and chains.

"The Daughters of the Maharajah; Princesses of the East!"

Each had long tresses of black hair and faces of beauty. One was the younger sister, wearing only a silk slip that barely hid her thin yet breathtaking frame and long, coltish legs. The elder tried only once to step in front of her sister before she was pulled back in place and had something whispered in her ear. She wore a set of lacey pink undies that loosely flowed off her ample breasts and hugged the roundness of her hips. She tried vainly to cover herself with her bound wrists, but she was yanked back slightly though firmly by her train of dark hair. While the M.C. described them, the ape displaying her took the opportunity to slip the tiny straps from her brassier off her shoulders, revealing dark nipples and bringing gasps of appreciation from the attending throng.

"Shall we begin the bidding at fifty thousand?"

The kidnapped daughters of the Maharajah were the crime that Crimson had been tracking to the event. If only he could also find Faustus among the throng. Nevertheless, the moment had come.

"Gentlemen," he strongly announced. He strode into the light, brandishing his blade and pistol. "This evening is at a close – the Maharajah's daughters are here illegally, kidnapped from their murdered father by Doctor Faustus and brought here to humiliate their uncle. You," he said pointedly while flashing his sword tip at the seated jackals, "are all here to be served."

He leveled his barrel at the biggest thug on the auction stage. "Justice." The giant bruiser standing beside the Indian girls blinked only once before Crimson fired. The bullet caught the man square in the chest and he fell backwards with a dying gasp.

All the slave girls screamed and ducked for cover, and the men closest to them stood for a confused moment, deciding whether to wrangle their property or run for their lives. Crimson took the moment to stab the closest one in the thigh with his blade, then shoot the first one that ran, felling him.

The eldest Indian girl grasped her shocked little sister and pulled her from the light, running from the stage. Crimson was too engaged to stop their flight immediately; he was stepping up to an approaching guard that had moved to attack him. He easily deflected the man's blackjack and ran him through to the hilt below the breast bone.

"Where's your master? Where's Faustus?" he demanded.

The guard only choked on blood-soaked spittle, but his eyes gave away the hiding place of his watching leader. Crimson pulled his short sword free and made for the curtained area behind the stage. He shot down two more henchmen as they approached, the second one just before he could raise a gun.

"The vengeance of the Crimson Cutlass is swift and sure, Faustus." Crimson ducked behind the curtains and rolled instinctively as a hail of bullets from a machine gun barely missed striking him in the head. He fired at the gunman, his pistol's barrels spinning, sending a burst of death. The man fell with a scream, a German machine gun slipping from his bloodied grip. The room was otherwise empty.

"Faustus!"

But only the sound of a closing door answered him.

Crimson ran towards the sound, turning a corner into room just as a hidden panel was slipping back into place over the door. Crimson reached for it but was knocked off his feet when the booby-trapped portal exploded. The Crimson Cutlass was saved by the hardwood pane that had concealed his enemy's flight. Even then, he was left pulling more than one large splinter from his flesh that night. He rolled over and got up after a moment of blurred vision and hearing loss, trying to shake off the effects of nearly being killed. When he could finally balance himself enough to kick aside what was left of the door, he could see that the secret elevator had already made its way to the ground floor. Faustus was gone.

He tried Mikey on his communicator fob, but he only got static - Faustus's escape was complete thanks to a jamming signal or some other interference.

Back in the ball room, Crimson found that Danny Walsh and Dr. Mifune had entered the room. Mifune covered the auctioneers and bidders that were either too slow or too incapacitated to escape with a rifle of his own design. Danny, local paperboy and agent of the Crimson Cutlass, was seeing to the girls. Even he had help; the Indian sisters had gone back to make certain their fellow kidnappees were alright after their awful ordeal. The princesses had already taken the time to cover themselves and the other girls.

"The police are on their way," Mifune announced. "You should leave now, sir."

Crimson turned to the princesses. "These girls will be well taken care of, you have my word. If you wish to escape here with as little known to the outside world as possible, then come with me now."

The eldest sister nodded after only a moment. "Yes, we shall come with you."

"Good," Crimson said, and motioned the way. "Your uncle is safe, and I can take care of you until you reunited are with family again, but I'm afraid it will take me time to find the man responsible for this."

"You mean...?"

"Yes - Dr. Faustus escaped."

Chapter 7

John and Genevieve walked into the compartment converted into a dining lounge for the evening, dressed in formal attire. The clipper's captain had invited the couple to dine with him at his table that evening. They smiled at a few other passengers and greeted the captain when he stood.

John shook his hand. "Captain Black; a pleasure. I'm Professor John Clark of Chicago. May I introduce Miss Genevieve Donovan, world-class traveler and activist."

"Ms. Donovan," the captain smiled. He was young, perhaps not yet thirty. Ruggedly handsome, the man had a Midwestern air about him. His suit was a double-breasted black affair, but his captain's hat was a stark white. "I'm Robert Black. Welcome aboard."

Genevieve smiled and they all sat. "Have you been flying the Pacific long, Captain?"

The captain paused to smile and unfolded his napkin. "Ah, well, long enough that I've been seriously considering going back to the mainland, though I would miss the tropics, to be sure. Well-traveled, are you both?"

"I used to see the world," Genevieve grinned. "This is my first excursion in some time."

"Mine as well," John agreed. "I've been out of the country a few times, but this is my first time to Hawaii."

"You'll love it," the captain said around a mouthful of fruit. His accent suggested perhaps the Midwest. He was still obviously excited by his job and its route.

The group talked and ate for a short while. John brought the conversation back to their destination. "In truth, Captain, we're just passing through Honolulu."

"Going on to one of the other islands, are you?"

"Yes," John paused, "and no. You see, we're looking for a stolen item, and we have reason to believe the thieves have taken it to a small island called Togabiza. I was hoping you might know where I..." John paused and looked at the beautiful but resourceful young woman beside him. "We," he corrected, "might be able to charter a pilot to take us there."

Captain Black's mood gained some seriousness and he used his napkin to carefully wipe his mouth. "I see," he said at last. "I'm sorry for your loss and hope that I can help at least peripherally." He motioned to a crew member waiting nearby. "My satchel, please, from the cockpit."

Soon the captain was opening a map he kept folded in his leather bag, scrutinizing the small islands of the South Pacific. "Togabiza," he murmured aloud. "Yes, I see." He set the map down. "You have to understand, Professor..."

"Please, call me John."

"Of course. John, you have to understand; for the most part, I just pass through this part of the world as I make my run. That said, I think I may know one or two guys who might be able to help you."

John nodded. "We would appreciate that, greatly."

"Depending on the size of aircraft you need and your timetable..." he trailed off. "Jake Cutter, out of the French Marivellas. He's a good seeming guy, flies a Grumman Goose perfect for island hopping. But you would have to wait a week to catch the clipper headed to Bora Gora."

"That's a long wait," John admitted. "And I'm not sure a Goose would be large enough to accommodate our stolen item, a large cabinet."

"I see." Captain Black sipped his coffee and raised an eyebrow. "Well, I know one other pilot who might be able to help. I'm not exactly friends with the guy, mind you, and he charges more but flies a bigger boat plane."

John smiled. "Money isn't a problem, and I think we can handle ourselves. Or is he a drunkard?"

The captain laughed. "No, just an egotist. Captain Donahue. I'll do my best to put you in contact once we reach Hawaii. Failing that, I'll leave contact information at your hotel for Mr. Cutter."

"Excellent, thank you," John replied. "We're staying at the Royal Hawaiian."

༺

The giant boat-plane docked at Pearl Harbor, and soon the young adventurers were having their luggage transferred to their room. They hailed a cab and soon they passed the Aloha Tower and were crossing the threshold of the stately Royal Hawaiian Hotel in Honolulu. John paused and took Genevieve's hand, standing with her in the sun.

Genevieve smiled at him. "What is it?"

John looked at the trees blowing in the tropical breeze. He looked up beyond the beach and buildings, to the mist hovering at the base of the swath of green rain forest covering the mountains. The ocean was a beautiful, clear blue rolling up the light sands and people were walking along the beach. "It's beautiful," he said. He took her in his arms. Genevieve laughed, and he kissed her. "You're beautiful. I wish we had more time."

She kissed him back, deeply. "We'll come back. I'm just glad we're together."

They spent the evening at the bar, enjoying cocktails while they waited

The Cabinet of Dr. Faustus

to hear from any of the contacts Captain Black had mentioned. The night air was still warm and lovely, so the pair took a walk along the beach, enjoying each other's company. It was approaching midnight, and Waikiki had grown quiet.

"I'm worried about Mary," Genevieve said.

John squeezed her hand. "I know. Me too."

"We don't even know if she's still alive."

He took her in his arms. John could feel her supple flesh through the thin material of her dress. He stroked her dark hair. He could feel the warmth of her body leaning against his linen clothes. Strong feelings of desire mingled with a protective instinct; here was a woman still so unknown to him and yet possessing so many qualities John never knew he was looking for, much less that a woman could have. She impressed him, and he wanted desperately to do whatever he could for her - to be witty for her. "We'll find her," was all he could promise.

Genevieve kissed him, tears streaming down her cheeks. The froth of sea foam swelled around their bare ankles as the tide washed ashore. "Make love to me," she said.

John almost moaned the answer to their desires into her mouth, but instead quietly embraced her with a mix of strength and subtlety. They rolled onto the sand and kissed deeply. She gasped, and he didn't know if it was from the evidence of his passion grinding between them, or the warm waters of the pacific splashing over her naked thighs. He pushed her dress up higher and sucked at her rounded peaks through the wet lace of her brassier. When his love filled her he could not help but groan his emotion into her ear at last.

"My love," she reciprocated.

The morning rays were warm and inviting. John heard the knock at the hotel room door a second time and untangled himself from the beautiful girl beside him, making certain the covers did her modesty justice. Even then, the sheets conformed to her nude body, revealing her perfect shoulders.

John wrapped himself in a robe. "Yes?"

"Professor Clark," came a voice. "Room service, sir - I have a message from the front desk."

John opened the door and took the message from the young man. "Thanks," he said, then fumbled for a tip from the trousers he'd left draped over a chair.

The door closed, and John opened the note.

Genevieve had stirred and looked inquisitive but well-rested. "Is it one of the pilots?"

"Captain Donahue," John nodded. "He's got a SARO A.27, he says."

"Which is?"

"A big damn boat plane." He winked wryly. "He can meet to discuss terms in two hours. I'll call the front desk, reserve us a meeting space."

"Good," she said, "two hours; that gives us a little time." Genevieve sat up and stretched, letting the covers fall to her waist. John watched the ripe sway of her perfect breasts, the morning air caressing their peaks to hardened points. She looked him in the eye and used one coltish leg to playfully kick the sheets onto the floor, revealing the rest of her nude body.

⁓

By the time the couple had dressed and prepared they had only five minutes to meet their party. John straightened the silk tie on his suit and ran his fingers through Genevieve's hair, down to the spaghetti straps of her light dress.

"Ready?"

She turned in his arms and deeply kissed him. "Yes." She breathed. "Let's go find Mary and get my cabinet back."

John nodded and stepped back. Each of them picked up their satchels. Genevieve's contained a sealed casket with the Chameleon's cloak inside; they hoped it might preserve the garment's invisibility long enough to complete their mission and recover the cabinet. John's satchel contained his own costume and weapons, making it a heavy if well-packed item, so he used its shoulder strap.

They walked to the lobby and spied a gruff if spry-looking man standing near the doors, a captain's cap held politely in his hands. His features suggested a British descent, with unshaven cheeks and a mess of sandy hair. He eyed the couple a moment as they approached, then smiled with an outstretched hand. "Professor Clark, Miss Donovan," he said, his accent solidifying John's assessment.

"Captain Donahue. Well met, sir."

"I understand," Donahue started with a scratching of stubble, "you're looking to charter me for a brief excursion."

"Yes, Captain." John motioned to the adjoining room he had reserved for privacy. "This way, please."

Once behind closed doors John said, "I understand you're flying a SARO A.27 seaplane, is that correct?"

"Yeah, gov." Donahue smiled and poured himself a glass of ice water.

Genevieve glanced at John and took up the next wave of the conversation. "We're on what we hope will prove to be something of a rescue mission, Captain. It's just the two of us heading to Togabiza, but if we're successful we'll be returning quickly with a third party and a large trunk."

"That sounds... interesting, ma'am." Donahue thought a moment. "But acceptable. Togabiza isn't too rough a haul. I'll calculate fuel costs separately." He passed a folded note to John. "That's my starting rate for this little adventure."

John glanced at the rate. "Done. When can we leave?"

~

Genevieve found her fingernails digging in to her seat's armrests as the boat plane banked low out of the clouds. The island of Togabiza was below them. At the steep angle in which they were banked, it seemed like she could fall straight down towards it through the window. She shook off the momentary vertigo.

Captain Donahue had to yell quite loud over the hum of his plane's engines. "There's your island, Professor. Look there, in the bay." He motioned, pointing at the crescent shaped inlet. There was another large boat plane beached against the edge of the jungle. Beyond it, the greenery gave way to mountains of black and gray volcanic rock. "Dornier Do24. That's a German plane."

Genevieve's eyes locked with John's and he nodded. "They're here," he said. "That's the same aircraft from the Chicago warehouse."

Donahue caught the exchange. "A little rescue mission, eh?"

"Please," Genevieve said, sensing the captain's reluctance. "We've come so far. We can't turn back now."

Donahue patted a holster hanging off his pilot's seat. "Don't you fret, Ms. Donovan. I've got ol' Bessie here. I'm on the level. But I'll be guarding the plane against those blighters." He glanced at their attire and simple cases they had brought along. "I just hope you two know what you're doing."

Donahue leveled off and traced the coastline, looking for a place to set down. "Chances are they've heard us pass over. I'll look for a spot we can beach and you can sneak in."

Genevieve felt John's hand caress the small of her back. "Strap in for the landing, darling," he said. "Then we'll get ready."

"It's hard not to get my hopes too high." Genevieve sat back down and listened to the quieting engine as the plane descended. "What's the plan?"

John was watching the darkening jungle through the plane's window. The dying light of day was already enveloping the lush green colors of the island. "I don't think that those Conclave bastards have been here long, so we can only hope there's just the group from the boat plane. But they came here with the cabinet for a reason, so we should assume there are others here in wait. In any case, we'll work our way to their landing and pick up the trail."

"Do you think we should capture some of them, get them to move the cabinet for us?"

John sighed. "I don't know. Everything I've seen makes me think otherwise; Faustus is an extremist, a political and strategic force outside the Nazi Party with his own agenda backed by an unseen foe. Whoever or whatever it is we saw on that screen at the warehouse, they could all be here. The Conclave of Three is confident and clandestine enough to work autonomously from Hitler. Whatever their plan is, if we can end it here..."

Genevieve found herself once more gripping her seat. The water rushed towards their view from inside the plane and soon it would be crashing against the hull as they landed in the water and powered their way to the island's coast. "I understand," she said, stiffening. "If Mary is there, alive, we save her. But either way..."

John nodded. "This ends tonight."

~

While Donahue was moving the boat plane towards the shore, Genevieve and John were beginning their transformation. Opening their cases, the pair began to change clothes. Stripped briefly to his boxers and undershirt, Genevieve gave John an appreciating smile. He left his linen pants on a seat, exchanging them for black trousers and the shirt with Crimson Cutlass's red skull emblazoned on it. He threw on his vest and belts with his weapon and tools holsters, placing his cloth mask under the tricorne hat until he was ready to don it. Genevieve pulled on black, skintight hose and tucked her light dress into them, giving John (and possibly Captain Donohue) the briefest glimpse of her tap pants. She pulled a black, sleeveless tank top on over her head before wrapping her thin torso in the Chameleon's corset and fastening the metal eyelets. She handed John her domino mask and gloves till she was ready, fastening her bullwhip to the hook on the corset's hip.

They were almost ready.

"I'll wait to pull out the cloak until it's time," she told John. "I don't know if it will last through the night. I've never had it out of the cabinet this long." Genevieve knew she looked fearful.

"We can do this, darling." He handed her a small pistol in a leather holster attached to a thin black belt. "Do you know how to use this?"

She resisted the urge to grumble. "If I have to."

"The clip holds six shots. There's a seventh in the chamber. The safety is on."

John picked up the bandolier and scabbard of his cutlass with one hand, steadying himself with the other when Donahue's plane hit the sand.

"We're here."

Donahue regarded them a moment, then got up from his seat. "I'll get the hatch," he said. Then he shook his head, reaching briefly for a nip from his flask before strapping on his own sidearm.

Genevieve placed her hands on her hips. "Keep some of that handy, captain Donahue," she said, eyeing the flask. "We may need it when we get back."

Donahue made no effort to hide a momentary wandering of gaze from her cleavage to her hips. Finally, he laughed. "Sounds promising, ma'am!"

Chapter 8

John stopped a few feet inside the cover of the jungle foliage and handed Genevieve her mask, tying on his own to cover his nose and mouth. His hat in place and bandolier strapped across his chest, once more he was the supreme visage of the Crimson Cutlass.

Genevieve pulled on her own mask and opera gloves, finally pulling her cloak out of a small, sealed case she'd kept hidden in a bag of sackcloth. Fastening the cloak at her throat, she pulled the hood up over her dark hair.

"The Chameleon returns," Crimson said with reverence.

She let out a worried breath. "Here's the real test." Gathering the cloak around herself, she gasped when the cloak did not immediately render her invisible. Within moments, though, the girl faded from view.

"It's okay - the cloak still works."

"For now," she said, returning to visibility. She rolled her eyes beneath a furrowed brow.

"We'll do the best with the hand we've been dealt, together." He placed a hand on her shoulder. "Come on, let's stay positive. I mean, we're only alone on a remote island in the South Pacific trying to rescue a girl from a band of über-Nazis and their shadowy leaders with only surprise and some choice weapons on our side - what could possibly go wrong?"

"You say the most wonderful things, darling."

"See?" he said and pulled the triple-barreled pistol from inside his great coat, cocking the first trigger into place. "I know how to talk to a gal."

The sun had passed behind the island's mountains, turning the green forest into deepening cool shades. Night was falling, bringing with it a sense of foreboding. It wasn't just the question of timing or finding the trail of where the Conclave members had gone. No, something else was in the air - the fiends were there for a reason, and they had to be stopped. Time was running out.

Chameleon sensed it too. "It's getting dark," she said. "I was thinking; if there is a guard at their plane, you feign getting captured and then I could follow, unseen. He'd lead us right to Mary and Faustus."

"I like that plan," Crimson said, "only he'd probably still be able to hear you hiking through this undergrowth."

She suddenly grasped his shoulder. "There!" she said, pointing. She lowered her voice despite the crashing waves on the beach a few yards away. "The German plane." Chameleon looked skyward. "Only a few minutes of daylight left."

"I don't see anyone," Crimson observed. "No movement, in or outside the aircraft. Let's get closer."

"No, let me go." And with that, the Chameleon wrapped her cloak about her form and was gone.

Crimson watched her tracks form in the sand, just barely discerning each tiny footprint in the gloom as she approached the large plane. It had been beached, pulled out from the water enough that one pontoon rested on the ground. He watched the surrounding area as she presumably checked within the plane, but no one was about. Crimson chanced to leave his cover of foliage and join her. By the time he was near the plane, Chameleon had revealed herself again.

"Nothing," she reported. "Even the pilot's gone with them. There's only a few supplies in the plane."

"Then they're here for the night, at least." Crimson looked along the beach and the jungle beyond. "There's our path."

A swath of vegetation had been chopped aside making a path leading into the jungle toward the mountain of lava rock still silhouetted against the gloom. The terrain climbed somewhat but looked easily traversable.

"The mountain," Chameleon murmured. "Or a cave within. We're gonna need a torch."

"Or a flashlight." Crimson pulled a small metal light from his pocket and flickered it on and off with a grin. "Come on. Our luck is holding."

~

Their shoes were speckled with mud from the rainforest floor and the path had turned steep leading up to the mountain, but otherwise the hike had been easy enough. Crimson Cutlass and Chameleon used the flashlight sparingly, hoping to retain an element of surprise.

Suddenly the path became stone beneath their feet.

"Rock," Crimson said, resisting the urge to mop the sweat from beneath the band of his hat. "I hope we don't have to climb much."

"Look, darling!" Chameleon pointed with one gloved finger towards the black abyss beyond the trees; a cave leading in to the heart of the mound. "It looks big enough. Think that they took the cabinet in there?"

Crimson nodded. "Time for your cloak to work its wonder, my dear - we're going in there."

The Chameleon donned the hood of her dark cloak and bodily faded from view. "Follow me," she whispered.

"Very funny." Crimson stepped forward, assuming he was trailing her small footfalls as they headed for the mouth of the cave. He was suddenly stopped by the sensation of the Chameleon's grip on his arm.

Her breath against his ear all but startled him. "Wait here."

The Crimson Cutlass was left standing alone at the edge of the jungle, her presence gone.

There was silence...

Until the outburst of an assaulted man's breath was preceded by the cracking sound of perhaps an uppercut to the jaw. A black-clad man fell backwards out of the cave and rolled down to land at Crimson's boots. The odd goggles with their markings denoted him as a member of Faustus' Conclave.

Crimson pulled some loose chord and a cloth from his pockets and began to bind and gag the unconscious fiend. "Nice work," he said, hoping that the Chameleon was within earshot. He looked up to see a floating German machine gun cradled in her invisible hands.

"I heard him click the safety off."

Crimson's eyebrows raised in appreciation of her. "Your senses are more acute than mine, darling."

"And I can teach you how to tread more quietly in those boots."

"How mystical." He nodded towards the cave. "Shall we? Are you comfortable with that Karabiner?"

"Only somewhat, and it makes me at least somewhat visible, or I could try to hide it beneath the cloak."

He unholstered his own specialized weapon. "Ok, let's go in, then."

The couple plunged into the darkness of the cave mouth and found themselves in a tunnel. Blackness enveloped them, so Crimson put out his hands and felt along the corridor, stumbling forward on the relatively easy terrain of the ancient lava tube. His shoulder bumped into the adjacent wall. "The tunnel is narrow here," he warned. Feeling around below and above him revealed much the same. "Damn."

"What?" she whispered.

"No way they got the cabinet through here."

The Chameleon sighed. "Maybe we missed a turn in the dark. They could have gotten the cabinet through another way."

"And they did leave a guard at the door," he reasoned.

"Look, ahead." He felt her tap his right shoulder. "I think I see light."

Again they crept forward through the cave. Further on, through the curtain of pitch, there was indeed a red haze. They moved forward without another word. The temperature began to climb from the cool moistness of the rock to an ominous heat.

The light grew in strength until the tunnel widened again and then opened up into a large cavern. Crimson found that they were up on a ledge overlooking the cave with a gradual incline to the floor below. A glowing pit in the center seemed to drop to a fiery chasm of lava, the churning orange mass of the volcano that further illuminated the cavern.

Crimson hung back to continue studying the scene.

A gasoline powered generator had been hooked to an observation lamp, with a second set of cables trailing to an assortment of odd equipment. Two men were near the machine, each dressed as members of the Conclave of Three. They were gesturing to two more of their ilk through a hole in the roof of the cave directly above the pit. The men there were working a suspended winch that was lowering Genevieve's cabinet down into the cavern.

Against one wall of the cave was a bound girl. It was Mary, stripped down to her satin undies and tied hand and foot, left to struggle against the ropes.

"At last," Crimson said. "We've found them."

"My God," said Chameleon.

Following what he presumed was her gaze, Crimson saw what had taken her breath away; another group of figures was across from Mary's position, surveying the scene with ominous quiet. One was similar to the other Conclave members in the room, a man dressed in black with a hood covering his face. The shroud was strapped on by a set of three-eyed goggles much like the others in his Conclave.

Dr. Faustus.

But behind him were three more figures - giants by normal standards, there was nothing human about these nearly naked monsters. Crimson recognized their basic shape as the same type of creature that had stood in silhouette with Faustus in the Chicago warehouse. Each was a hulking beast with dark, greenish skin and three bulbous, black eyes. These alien creatures had massive shoulders with long, sinewy arms tapering down to lanky hands with only three fingers each.

"I think we've found the real masters behind the Conclave of Three."

Chameleon swallowed audibly. "What are they?"

The very question shattered Crimson's perceptions of reality and sent his mind reeling. He could fathom answers, but none of them was anything he was willing to say aloud for trepidation of making his fears a reality.

After a pause, he said, "Whatever they are, they look mean, and hard to kill."

"*These* things are in league with Hitler?" the Chameleon asked in disbelief. "My God, how do we warn the world?"

One of the creatures was speaking to Dr. Faustus, it's alien maw an awful grin of fangs and a slavering forked tongue. Faustus answered briefly, then spoke to his minions louder in his native German dialect. With that, one of the Conclave thugs turned to the nearly nude form of Mary and picked her struggling body up. He began to approach his masters with her presented in his arms.

"Right," Chameleon said, "we've got to stop them, whatever they're doing. I'll move closer. As soon as I get Mary out of the line of fire, you take over. I'll cover you once the shooting starts."

"Good; you have more bullets than I do." Crimson shook his head but smiled. "A rough plan is still a plan, I guess." He looked at her pretty eyes when Chameleon's face emerged briefly from the darkness of her cloak to kiss his lips. She hid her face and the German's machine gun beneath her cloak and he felt her move past him. "Good luck."

"You too."

Crimson checked his own weapons. The saber at his side was a formidable weapon, but he didn't plan on getting close enough to use it. He custom pistol with the triple barrels had an attachment or two he could bring into play as needed. Until then, his current placement afforded him a view with decent cover, so he would rely on his accuracy for picking off his first targets.

But all his plans went to hell in the next moment... when he realized he could see the Chameleon as she snuck towards the cave floor.

Her cloak's abilities were powered by the very cabinet that it had not recharged in for days, and now the effect was wearing thin. The Chameleon wasn't completely visible - the effect was more like a moving shadow gliding across the dimly lit cavern, but the closer she got to the main floor, the more obvious she was.

Crimson swore.

He could only watch and hope that their enemies were too preoccupied to notice her. The cabinet was being lowered from the roofline towards the pit, but Crimson had stopped wondering what the fiends were up to. Fastening his length of chord to the grappling hook he'd unfolded from his belt, he prepared to hook the assembly to his pistol for the inevitable.

Crimson looked down just in time to see the Chameleon's shadow finally leap to the main floor and begin running in the direction of the soldier carrying Mary. She was halfway to them when the first Conclave member shouted, pointing.

"*Mein Gott!*"

Machine guns were unstrung and leveled at the shadowy form.

Chameleon paused, realizing she had been made. Faustus bellowed something and the remaining Conclave member on the ground moved towards her, motioning with his gun barrel. Barking orders in German, it was clear he knew exactly where she was.

He took several rounds in the chest from Chameleon's machine gun for his troubles.

The barrels on Crimson's pistol rotated as he seized the moment, shooting the two men on the winch above. His accuracy was pretty good considering he was shooting through a hole in the roof from an angle; he plugged one right in the chest and the man slumped aside, screaming. The second took a slug in the leg as he maneuvered for a clear shot. He slipped on his own bleeding limb and scrambled to catch the edge of the roof, but to no avail. The Conclave brute bounded off a corner of the cabinet as he dropped, but it didn't check his fall enough to land him safely below. Instead, he careened through the hole to the pit beneath the ancient box, plunging to a charred death.

Crimson turned his aim towards Faustus, but he never got off the ground. There was a flash of green light from a weapon held by one of the alien creatures, and the rock to Crimson's left exploded, sending him flying.

Chapter 9

The Conclave soldier that was carrying Mary had dropped her in the fray and moved back towards Chameleon the moment she had shot the first man. By the time she had trained her gun to his direction, he had already moved close enough to bat the barrel away and tackle her to the ground. The gun fell from her grip as she was pushed to the cave floor and her head met rock. The Chameleon looked over to where a flash of strange light had made an explosion of rock near Crimson's position. Just before she lost consciousness, she could see her lover's prone form on a ledge, blood seeping from a wound on his scalp.

~

When she came to she was bound, her wrists tied behind her back and her cloak had been removed. Mary was beside her. They were sitting against a rock near the center of the cavern. Her weapons were gone, except the whip at her side.

"Oh, thank God you're alright," Mary said.

The hooded man the Chameleon knew must be the mysterious Dr. Faustus turned from where he was surveying the winch, her cloak draped over his arm. He spoke with an accent at once German, and yet tainted by something else. "Ah, Miss Donovan. At last. You're just in time to see the birth of a new world."

The Chameleon shook off her stupor as best she could, but the unease of dread and the splitting headache did little for her demeanor. "Dr. Faustus, I presume," was all she managed. She mentally smiled at the witticism in the face of death, then began surveying her surroundings. From where she had been placed there wasn't much to see. If Crimson was still on the ledge where he had fallen, she couldn't even see his body, much less whether he might still be alive. She fought back panic and tears.

"I am pleased," said Faustus. "In spite of your transgressions, 'Chameleon', you have provided yourself as another gift to my masters. When this experiment has concluded, you will both return with them to their place amongst the stars. But not before they have attained a new power, tonight!"

The Chameleon and Mary glanced at each other and shuddered at the prospect. "What are those things?" her friend said, shrinking away.

Faustus spread his arms wide. "The new Masters of Earth, child, that is what they are. Beings from another world, here to conquer this one. Let Hitler's armies stampede across nations until his resources dwindle. Soon, it won't matter who thinks they control humanity - when my Masters invade, all will fall to their might. I have seen it! And you, Miss Donovan, have given us yet another advantage in the coming storm."

Her cabinet had been lowered to the floor near her and the three grotesque creatures were examining the ancient box. Strange metal devices had been fastened to it by them, and two were making adjustments while the third had opened the door and was stepping inside. Once more, the Chameleon heard their alien voices as they gestured to each other, then the one inside closed the door. The winch started up, and the cabinet and its occupant were pulled slightly aloft, then maneuvered back over the shaft to the chamber below. They slowly began to lower their comrade down.

The Chameleon struggled in vain against her bonds. "No! What are they doing?"

Faustus laughed. "How typical of such a lesser human. You do not think past what you see. Do not worry, Miss Donovan - we would not dare harm your precious cabinet. We have simply modified its use." He dropped her cloak near Chameleon's feet. She took the opportunity to tuck her boots closer to her bound hands, reaching for the knife secreted within.

"How the cabinet came to those who gave it to your family I do not know," Faustus continued, "but somehow they were at least able to harness its basic power. The foundation for the cabinet was what you might term as a falling star, though the meteor was more like a perfect geode. The minerals within are not of this world, Miss Donovan, though perhaps you guessed at such a concept each time you used it to give you a cloak of invisibility. How crude," he snorted.

The winch stopped.

"My master within the cabinet will not have to withstand the heat for long. He is only low enough for the unique properties of the cave of molten rock to have their own effects on our technology and the cabinet's abilities. Now - now it is a device of *true* power!" Faustus stomped excitedly back to where the girls waited and crouched down before them. Training the three lenses of his mask on the Chameleon he gripped her by the neckline of her bodice. She winced at the strength of his gloved fingers pressed against her cleavage, threatening to tear her costume. "At last, child! My search for your geode cabinet ends and the might of my masters and their technology will change the future of everything. Don't you see it?" He laughed. "No, you do not."

The winch started up again, raising the steaming cabinet back up from the lava cave and setting it back near the edge of the abyss.

"How could you see, puny woman?" Faustus used his gloves to open the doors to the augmented cabinet, swinging them wide to reveal... emptiness. Faustus reached towards where the figure of the alien creature had stood within the box, and his hand met an invisible resistance. He laughed. "For now, fool, you find that my master is invisible."

A horrid laugh began, beginning with the alien voice inside the cabinet, and echoed by its two compatriots standing nearby. The laughing reverberated around the cave, and the Chameleon froze with terror.

Faustus turned and pulled off his mask, revealing a horribly twisted and smiling visage of something part man, part creature. The three black eyes of the monstrous face of the half-breed Dr. Faustus regarded the Chameleon and her shivering, naked friend. A forked tongue snaked over twisted lips. "My masters and I will build an invisible army," he announced, "and nothing will stand in our way!"

The air was shattered by the single, booming shot of a gun.

One of the aliens gurgled and clutched at his eyes, but all three had been pierced by a buckshot round from the inimitably unique gun of the Crimson Cutlass.

Chameleon smiled and turned to see Crimson just as he literally swung into action by a rope and hook he'd grappled to the winch. The arc of his swing took him within kicking distance of Faustus, sending him sprawling. In that same moment Crimson fired again, striking the first alien in the head a second time. The beast fell, its screams cut off.

The other visible creature narrowly avoided Crimson's swing. It pulled a metallic gun from a sidearm holster and fired another round of its blinding ray. Crimson avoided the blast and took a moment to toss a knife to the Chameleon. "Here!"

"Unnecessary, my love," she said, cutting through the last of her ropes with her secret blade. "But I'll take the second knife anyway." She grunted as she broke free and stood, spinning to throw the blade at Faustus where he had fallen. The dazed half-breed rolled, and her throw missed. Faustus pulled a long dagger from his own belt and stood.

The Chameleon picked up Crimson's knife and helped Mary stand in one motion, beginning to cut her free as they ran from the field of battle. "Hurry!"

Crimson had bolted for the cover of rock, but it was being diminished by each blast from the alien ray. "Destructive your weapon may be," Crimson called out to his foe. He leapt from his position and rolled, coming up to fire several repeating shots into the giant black eyes of his opponent. The creature screeched and fell. "But aiming is an acquired skill."

The Chameleon sawed through Mary's ropes and pointed at the safety of rock. "Go, there!" She unfastened her bullwhip from the belt around her corset and snapped at the interior of her cabinet. The whip only struck

The Cabinet of Dr. Faustus

empty air. "Crimson, there's still one more!"

"I know!"

"Imbeciles!" Faustus jumped an amazing distance and stabbed at Crimson, nearly skewering him. "You cannot stop the coming storm! *We* shall be Masters of Earth!" He jabbed and knocked the gun from Crimson's hand.

Chameleon froze, expecting the worst, but her beloved drew his blade and barely managed to turn aside the next stab of Faustus' dagger.

"At last, I'll have the chance to kill you, Faustus."

"One chance is all you'll get." He parried and thrust at the Crimson Cutlass, nearly stabbing his foe yet again. "I was trained by fencing masters a hundred years before you were born!" Their blades clashed.

Even as the Chameleon watched the scene unfold she knew her own life was hardly out of danger. She picked up a German Luger pistol from a dead Conclave guard and ran for her cloak, still lying where Faustus had dropped it. She knelt and donned the long garment, pulling the hood up over her dark hair.

Chameleon barely had a moment to concentrate enough to change the weakened cloak less opaque, partly concealing her. The moment was in vain - the invisible form of the last alien creature slammed into her bodily, sending her sprawling. She rolled and came up firing but hit nothing. Pulling free her whip once more, she began randomly spinning it to test proximity. She inched forward with her gun at the ready, waiting for the moment to shoot whatever the whip might connect with. She could only hope that her love was faring better. She chanced a look.

Crimson brought his cutlass down, nearly cutting Faustus in half, but the creature possessed incredible strength, and stopped the cut midair with his dagger. Faustus gripped Crimson's extended wrist with his free hand and disengaged his dagger, lashing out. Crimson twisted his body away, unable to break free, and the blade connected with his chest and shoulder. His leather baldric and coat took most of the cut, but the dagger still bit into flesh and he cried out. Shifting his weight to his left boot, he kicked Faustus in the gut with his right, breaking loose of his grasp.

Spinning, Crimson lashed out with his sword again, but Faustus parried easily and jabbed, nearly gutting him. He stepped back, deflecting another lightning-quick set of jabs with each retreating step.

"How typically weak," Faustus sneered. "Your kind will be mowed down like wheat. Even Hitler's army will fall before the might of my masters."

Rocking back on his heel, Crimson evaded another attack and changed his stance, stabbing forward and extending his arm while balancing on flexed knee. The assault worked and Faustus froze, staring at the inches of steel buried in his chest. All three eyes blinked once, then he collapsed.

Crimson pulled his cutlass free as his foe toppled. "You impressed me, Faustus," he spat. "But not much."

He screamed when three unseen claws raked across his back, opening cuts in leather as well as flesh.

"Perhaps I impress you more, human."

Flashes and the banging report of a pistol went off directly beside the disembodied alien screech. The creature fell, its giant body fading back into view as the bullets in its side broke its concentration.

The Chameleon removed her hood and aimed down at the injured thing she had blindsided. "How did you miss me with eyes that big?" She emptied the rest of the Luger's clip into the giant, insectoid eyes of the alien monster, turning them into gory pools. The creature lay silent.

"John! My God, John, are you alright?" Genevieve pulled off her mask and worked to free Crimson's as well, careful not to touch his injured back. She turned his face to look at her. "John!"

"That... really hurt."

Relieved, she knelt close and kissed his face. "You're something. Can you move?"

John groaned and sat up in her arms. "I'm something? You're the one that saved my bacon!"

"After you saved all of ours." Mary came over and joined them, hugging her friends. They all looked over at the cabinet sitting near the smoking cavern of lava.

John sighed. "I am not looking forward to carrying that thing."

~

"You two get into some weird shite." Donahue handed John his flask. "Here, gov', as promised."

Genevieve brought Captain Donahue and some clothes for Mary back from the plane and to the base of the cave mount. By then, John and Mary had employed the winch to lift the cabinet back up from inside the cave and then used a sled the Conclave had brought to slide it back down from the top of the slope to the edge of the jungle. The four people were then able to lift and carry it back to the boat plane. Soon the exhausted crew were all aboard and flying back to the Hawaiian Islands.

John held Genevieve close as they drifted in and out of sleep in their seats.

"Those things," Genevieve began.

"I know. I almost don't want to talk about them for fear of bringing more. If Faustus was right..."

"What do we do, John? Who do we tell?"

"Its questions we can leave for another day. Perhaps I'll bring Dr. Mifune back to the cave to examine the remains. In the meantime, we can only hope that their numbers are small and that is why they needed the power of invisibility."

Genevieve nodded against his chest. "I love you, John. Tell me we'll never be apart."

He looked into her eyes. "We'll never be apart, my love."

Epilogue

The following week the couple spent in Hawaii, enjoying their wait for the next clipper. John arranged for the cabinet to be shipped to his mansion outside of Chicago.

Their time amongst the beaches and forests of Oahu were bright and lovely. The couple married in Honolulu and treated their time as a proper honeymoon. Mary was witness and spent the occasion with her friends on the sands of Waikiki. By the time the clipper pulled into port at Pearl City, the trio had all but washed away the harrowing days before.

"Captain Black!" John shook the pilot's hand as they boarded, glad to see a familiar face.

Robert Black smiled and took in the couple and their friend. "Can I assume that your mission to the South Pacific was a success?"

"Indeed, Captain." Genevieve smiled when Robert kissed her hand. "And how fair you?"

"Well. Oh, I see we have changed a few things!" he exclaimed at the ring. "*Mrs. Clark*, I presume." She nodded with a smile. "Well, my mainland friends, this will be my last flight as the captain of the clipper. I think it's time to stick to more landlocked locales. The East is becoming... bumpy."

"I think the future holds many hardships, Captain Black," John said. Aboard the plane, he pulled the captain aside. "Germany and the Far East aren't the only concerns we have as men."

"You believe war is on the horizon?" Robert Black's brow creased.

John didn't answer. After a moment he reached into his bag and pulled free a Mauser, one of the items he had collected from the fallen Conclave of Three. He tried not to think of the other strange things he had seen on Togabiza.

Three eyes. Three fingers. Hulking beasts with forked tongues.

"Take this, Captain. Go home - protect your own. I think the world will soon be a much smaller place."

End

About the Author

Scott P. 'Doc' Vaughn is a Phoenix illustrator and writer, originally hailing from Wisconsin. When he's not hard at work on comics and commissions, he's trying hard to catch up on drawing his web-comic creation, *Warbirds of Mars*. Some of Doc's fantasy pen and ink art was featured in *A Life of Ravens: Epic Poetry and Narrative* and *Lancelot: Poems About the Man and Legend* by Alex Ness, and in *The Crypt of Dracula* by Kane Gilmour. Among Doc's interests are classic illustrations and movie genres, vintage clothes and cars, pulp magazines, and a severe predilection for *Doctor Who* since the age of eight. He lives in a very classic house with a cat, a bird, and occasionally a dog. Visit him at http://www.vaughn-media.com.

THE ADVENTURE CONTINUES! IN THE ORIGINAL WEBCOMIC
FROM SCOTT P. 'DOC' VAUGHN AND KANE GILMOUR
THAT STARTED IT ALL!

WARBIRDS OF MARS

WWW.WARBIRDSOFMARS.COM

COMIC BOOKS! T-SHIRTS! RADIO SHOWS! & MORE!

WARBIRDS OF MARS
STORIES OF THE FIGHT!

SEAN ELLIS

RON FORTIER

STEPHEN M. IRWIN

J. H. IVANOV

DAVID LINDBLAD

JEFFREY J. MARIOTTE

ALEX NESS

CHRIS SAMSON

MEGAN E. VAUGHN

AND MORE

EDITED BY
SCOTT P. VAUGHN & KANE GILMOUR

WWW.WARBIRDSOFMARS.COM

HERO·LORE

SHARDS OF DESTINY
BOOK I OF THE HERO·LORE

SCOTT P. VAUGHN

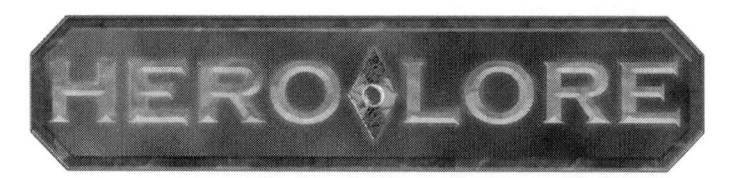

A SCI-FI/FANTASY ADVENTURE NOVEL

COMING SOON

WWW.HERO-LORE.COM

WWW.VAUGHN-MEDIA.COM

Made in the USA
Columbia, SC
15 May 2020